W9-BSA-447

The Boy and the Samurai

The Boy and the Samurai

Erik Christian Haugaard

Houghton Mifflin Company
Boston 1991

Library of Congress Cataloging-in-Publication Data

Haugaard, Erik Christian.

The boy and the Samurai / Erik Christian Haugaard.

p. cm.

Summary: Having grown up as an orphan of the streets while sixteenth-century Japan is being ravaged by civil war, Saru seeks to help a Samurai rescue his wife from imprisonment by a warlord so they can all flee to a more peaceful life.

ISBN 0-395-56398-4

[1. Japan—History—Period of civil wars, 1480-1603—Fiction.] I. Title.

PZ7.H286Bn 1991 90-47535

[Fic]—dc20 CIP

AC

Printed in the United States of America

AGM 10 9 8 7 6 5 4 3 2 1

For my grandson, Adam

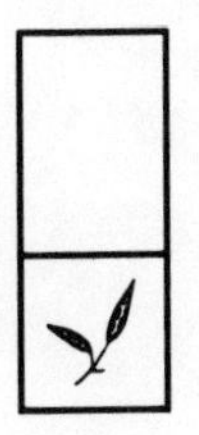

Contents

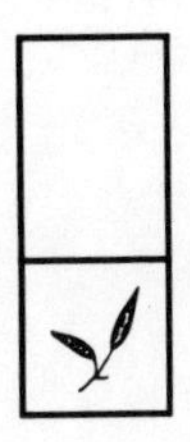

List of Characters

Lord Takeda Katsuyori
The cruel lord of the province of Kai.

Lord Oda Nobunaga
Ruthless warlord and enemy of Katsuyori.

Lord Uesugi Kenshin
Ruler of the province of Echigo. An enemy of Katsuyori.

Lord Tokugawa Iyeyasu
A warlord and enemy of Katsuyori.

Saru
Hero and narrator of the story, son of a soldier who died in battle.

Lord Akiyama Nobutora
An old Bushi who befriends Saru.

Jogen
A kindly priest in a small temple who takes Saru in.

Murakami Harutomo
A Samurai whose wife is held captive by Katsuyori.

Aki-hime
His wife.

Shiro
A young thief and sometime friend of Saru.

Haru-san
The kindhearted owner of a soba shop.

Yosaku
A crippled thief.

Nezumi
Leader of a gang of young thieves.

Nami
The young daughter of a cook in Katsuyori's kitchen and a good friend to Saru.

Sumi-san
An old crone, owner of an inn.

Ojiisan
An old man with a youthful spirit.

Kura
A strange lame girl who lives with Haru-san.

Aya-san
A poor woman who takes care of the very young Saru.

Matsu
Her little daughter.

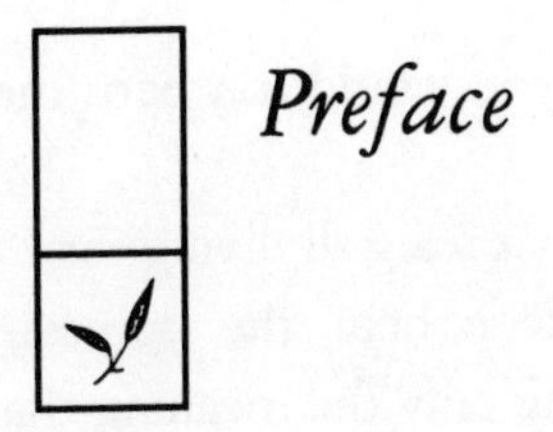

Preface

"Spring will soon be here. I saw a bird flying with twigs in its beak to build its nest with. Another year is gone. The older we get, the more our lives resemble a circle." As he spoke, my friend the priest looked out over the sea which stretched beneath us, blue and still, to the horizon. I looked back toward the temple. The winter winds had made it even more weatherworn, perched as it was on a bank close to the sea.

"Harutomo-san, are you happy now?" I asked him. "Do you sometimes wish that you had not shaven your head and become a priest? That, in your obi, were still the two swords of the Samurai?"

"Sometimes in the night, when darkness has hidden the world, I dream of the past. Then again I wear the two swords that it took me so long to earn. But when I wake and the stillness of the morning is only broken by the sound of the waves playing upon the stones on the beach, then I think that I was wise to stay here. But what about you, Saru? Priest Jogen wanted you to be a priest. They were his last words to me when he was dying. He was a true friend to you. But you refused as always, saying that you would stay Saru the monkey. Are you happy now?"

"I am contented. Look at that sea gull diving for a fish. Is it happy if it catches it? I like it here, the stillness of the nights, the long days containing only the meaning that I can give them. Like you, I sometimes dream of the past, of all the dangers that I encountered and all the people I once knew."

"I, too, Saru, am contented, and that brings peace. One life contains many lives. I once wrote down the story of my youth. The tale of the young Samurai. Then, as my brush touched the paper, the past became alive to me again, the beauty and the horror of that time. You, Saru, should do the same—tell the story of Saru the monkey."

I smiled and shook my head. "I fear that I would not tell it truthfully, nor write it well enough. My hand would shake, and the ink blot the paper."

"Saru, you know that you wield the brush like a master. Write it truthfully, as I told the tale of my youth."

As my friend spoke I thought of my childhood. Yes, it contained a story worth telling. Pictures appeared in my mind. The one that stayed the longest was of a girl who had been a member of a little band of robbers who had all, except for her, been killed. I recalled her sitting on the floor of the hovel that had been their quarters. She was staring at a dried puddle of blood.

"As I wrote the tale of my youth, I relived it with each stroke of the brush. When I had finished I felt that a burden had been taken from me . . . I felt at ease with myself."

Harutomo-san paused, searching for words. "Maybe I needed to write it down, to find myself . . . maybe to like myself."

"To like yourself?" Puzzled, I repeated his words.

"If you don't, life can become a burden too heavy to bear." Seeing the confusion mirrored on my face, he laughed and added, "But you can only truly like yourself once you have admitted to what you are. Recalling deeds which you might not be proud of. The glory of truth is that it sets you free. A liar must forever lie."

"Some people like to shout about their misdeeds as if they were proud of them," I said, picking up a little stone and trying to throw it as far as the sea. It fell among the pebbles on the beach.

"I have no respect for those who come here and knock their heads against the floor in front of Buddha, telling him all about their sins. A man who makes himself out to be a greater villain is as foolish as those who brag about their virtues. Truth must be sought for its own sake."

"Am I nearer to knowing the truth now than I was then?" I asked. "The young dream about the future and the old about the past."

Harutomo-san laughed. "Most old Samurais sharpen their swords in their dreams. When you listen to one retelling the story of some famous battle he claims to have fought in, do not believe him. More often than not, he is lying as fast as the fleetest horse can run."

"Then we shall never know the truth." I felt the warmth of the sun through my thin clothing.

"We can do no more than attempt to tell the truth." Harutomo-san smiled and looked at me. "Do that, Saru, and your tale will be worth listening to."

Suddenly I realized that I would do so, that I was eager to do so. I thought of my little room in the temple, my desk and my brushes and my ink stone. Still I objected.

"Where, and how, do I start?"

"At the beginning, that is always the wisest." Harutomo-san rose. "We have lived in an evil time but one that will be talked about when better days are fast forgotten."

He walked away, and I knew where he was going: to pray at the grave of his wife, who died a few years before and was buried beyond the temple. To begin at the beginning, that was sound advice. The beginning for all of us is our birth, so with that I shall start my tale.

The Boy and the Samurai

1 In Which I Tell of My Birth and How I Became an Orphan

The exact date when I came into the world I do not know. It was in the spring, five years before the great warlord Takeda Shingen, the ruler of the province of Kai, died. I seem to have had my doubts about the desirability of being born, as I finally had to be cut from my mother's womb. My mother did not survive my birth by more than a few hours, which left my father in a most precarious position. What was he to do with this bloody little piece of humanity, which whimpered and cried and claimed to be his son? He was not a rich man who could send a servant to fetch a wet nurse; if such was wanted he had to find one himself. He wrapped me in a blanket and set forth toward that part of the city of Kofuchu nearest the river. A friend of his lodged there, and he knew that a child had been born in that house a few days before.

Aya-san took one look at me, put me to her breast, and told my father that she was not running a free orphanage. He took out his purse, which contained only copper coins, and, peering into it, drew forth one. Aya-san looked down at me drinking greedily and held up five fingers. With a sigh, my father handed her four more coins.

"Each month," Aya-san said, slinging me across her shoulder and patting my back until I burped.

My father nodded, took one last look at me, then went to see his friend and invited him to partake in some sake at a nearby tavern. The two of them celebrated my birth until my father's purse was as empty as the sake bottles it had purchased. Then he went home to arrange my mother's funeral.

I do not know if my mother had wanted me. She may have, but certain it was that no one else did. To Aya-san I was five copper coins a month but also a lot of trouble. To my father I was an expense he could ill afford, and to the rest of the world I was nothing at all. To Aya-san's daughter, Matsu, I was a thief who stole half, if not more, of her mother's milk. No, I was not wanted! But if only the children who were wanted lived, there would be fewer people in this world. Mindless of this, I sucked at Aya's breasts, thrived, and grew fat. By the time I was a year old I could walk out into that world which did not care about me.

The world grows bigger and bigger as you grow yourself. At first Aya-san was all I knew and needed, then Matsu entered it, for we shared the same corner of the room. We were loyal to each other. When one cried the other immediately joined in. This resulted either in our being slapped or taken up and allowed to suck. As we grew older and hungrier, and therefore cried more often, we were usually slapped. Soon we learned that crying was not the only way of communicating with the strange world around us. We learned to make noises which were at least sometimes understood by the giants who took care of us. We both learned to talk at about the same age, and also to lie. For to lie is a very necessary accomplishment if you want to survive. Now lying is not a matter only of using words. Sounds, or even facial expressions, may serve as well. In this way one learns to lie before one can talk. I am sure I was well able to lie before I had understood that sounds could be formed into words. When Aya-san smacked me I howled as if she were taking my life away, even when it didn't hurt, for I knew that only when I howled loud enough would she stop. Like most grownups, Aya-san was a person of moods. What deserved a slap one moment might pass unnoticed the next, or even be rewarded with a hug. Her husband had been a foot soldier until an arrow in his leg made him lame. He became a seller of charcoal, a fact that only a blind person might miss, for his face—and most of the rest of him—was as black as his wares. Our house was near the river. It was very small and built from timber the charcoal seller had bought when an old house had been torn down. Sometimes the houses built nearest the river were swept away by floods, and often their owners were drowned. Then there would be a lot of screaming and crying by the survivors, and with tear-stained faces they would go to pray to Buddha. The temples were never built so close to the river that they were in any danger. But not long after, new shacks were built on the same land, for the poor live only for today and tomorrow is almost as far away as next year.

When I was four years old Lord Takeda Shingen won a great victory (over Lord Tokugawa Iyeyasu) at a place called

Mikata-ga-hara. A great celebration was held in the castle, but down by the river there was less reason to rejoice. Though Takeda Shingen had won a victory, others had not. My father had met a personal defeat, dying in the early part of the battle. A spear had penetrated his chest. This, I was told, proved that he had died bravely, facing the enemy. As I was only four years old, I did not mourn my father. Aya-san did, or rather, mourned the five copper coins which she would receive no more. Aya-san was poor, so poor that often she went hungry, yet she did not throw me out when I became a burden in place of an income.

The fact that I was now an orphan changed my life in one respect. I had, so to speak, been demoted. Whereas, previously I was considered superior to Matsu, who was merely a girl, I now ranked below her. Now she got the bigger portions of food and I the smaller. Thus I came to realize the importance of having parents. I was often told that they ought to carry me up into the mountains and leave me as food for the wild animals or Yamamba. Yamamba is a witch who lives in the mountains and eats children when she catches them. Somehow this never frightened me. I did not believe that Aya-san would do such a thing, and the mountains were far away. But I did feel that somehow the fact of being an orphan was my fault, as if I had lost my parents by negligence. I often dreamed that my father had not been killed in the battle but returned to me. As I had no memory of what he looked like, he appeared in my dreams in the dress of a wealthy Samurai. This shows that very early on I had a sense of what is important in life. There would have been very little point in dreaming of a missing father who appeared in rags with a beggar's bowl in his hand.

The following year Takeda Shingen died and his son Katsuyori became master of Kai. I was by then five years old and the territory which I considered my own had been enlarged to contain the whole part of the city near the river. I was always hungry and therefore ever looking for means to fill my belly. Begging was not profitable since everyone was poor around our house. Stealing was difficult but could be done, though not without the risk of a beating if caught. The death of the lord of our province made no impression upon me. In my world Aya-san was the only lord who was important to have as a friend, not Takeda Katsuyori. I never learned her husband's name. He was a man of very little importance in our household, where he seldom even appeared. He made his home in a small sake tavern in the next street, and the woman who ran that received more of his profits than Aya-san. Sometimes Matsu and I were sent over there with messages for him. The woman who ran the tavern was very fat and would give us rice cakes. I found all this normal, even the hunger in my belly, for children adapt themselves to changing conditions more easily than grownups.

The year when I was six years old the summer was particularly dry. No rain fell at all, and the river became a mere trickle. Now if flooding was one danger to the part of the town near the river, fire was the second. How the fire started I do not know. There had been an earthquake that night and a candle might have tipped over. I woke up in the middle of the night to find it was bright as day. I heard the crackling of the flames and woke Matsu, who slept next to me. Aya-san was awake, too, and had gathered her valuables into a little bundle. She took Matsu by the hand, and we ran from the house. The sky was red as blood and the sound of the fire, like a hungry tiger eating the timber of the houses, was terrifying. There were people everywhere, running in different directions like frightened chickens. I ran toward the river as fast as my little legs could carry me. Once I stumbled and fell and a man kicked me, but I was up almost immediately. The dried riverbed was teeming with people, most of them carrying bundles containing their most precious possessions. Some were calling out the names of friends or family members whom they had lost in their flight from the flames. I ran from one group to another looking for Aya-san and Matsu, but they were nowhere to be found. They must have run in the wrong direction and been caught by the fire.

By midafternoon, when the flames had died down, I began to realize that I would never see Aya-san or Matsu again. Now I was truly an orphan, without family or friends. I had lived only six years but experienced enough misfortunes in that short time for me to expect little from fate but more hard knocks.

Our house was nothing but ashes. I poked among them with a stick and found an unbroken bowl. It was just the right size for a beggar's bowl. I cleaned it as best I could, then went to a temple and begged the priest for some food. There were other beggars there as well and only a little millet, so my portion was very small. One cannot remember one's own birth, but I shall never forget this, my second "birth," and it is from that day that I truly reckon my life.

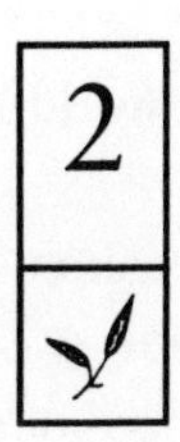

2 A Child as Valuable as a Cockroach

Some believe that you are punished in your next life if you misbehave in your present one. It is said that misers who lend out money at high interest become cockroaches when they die. If this is true, I surely must have done some evil deeds in my former life to have ended up as miserable as I was after the fire, at six years old a double orphan, having lost not only my parents but my foster mother, too. No door in the whole city would open to let me in. No roof would shelter me.

So far I have not mentioned my name. Naturally, I had one, or people would not have been able to curse me when I got in their way. The most insignificant things have names, even when they don't deserve them. On that night when I was born, my father was too troubled to bother about such a thing as a name. If he gave me one later, I never learned of it. I was given a name by Aya-san's husband, the seller of charcoal. It was not one I would have chosen myself. Saru—monkey—he called me, and the name stuck or fitted me so well that I was not given another one.

Although it was summer and the weather was hot, I looked for a place which I could make my home. To sleep under the sky is frightening—one wants the world to have walls and a ceiling once the sun has set.

Twice, with great difficulty, I managed to collect a small pile of timber to make a shelter, but each time it was stolen, probably by someone in as much, or greater, need of a house than I was. I doubt that I would have been able to build anything out of it had I been allowed to keep it. I had no tools and no knowledge of how to use them if I had had some.

A priest at a small unimportant temple had gotten so used to seeing me that he fed me like a stray animal. It was the season of fruits, and the temple was well supplied with them. Like any homeless cat or dog, I had so much trouble filling my belly each day that I had no time to think of the future or to fear it. There would have been good reason to do so, for in the autumn the nights grow cold as the snow falls in the mountains. It would have been wise of me to search for a shelter before the winds started to undress the trees.

When I did find one, it was purely by chance. Not very far from the temple where the priest was kind enough to feed me, there was a small shrine to Oinari-sama. It was built of wood and very shabby, and few people worshipped there. Oinari-sama is the god of rice and has two foxes who serve him. The foxes carry messages, and one of them has a roll of paper in his mouth. It is well known that foxes, as well as Tanuki the Badger and the Crane, can change themselves into human beings if they want to. I liked the little fox god and felt that he was nearer to being a child like myself, so I would sometimes pray to him. He is fond of fried bean curd and sake too.

Many Buddhists think little of Oinari-sama, though I believe he is a very ancient god. The people who worship him are by many considered simple; they are often poor or very young. That fall when I was six I had great faith in the power of the fox, and it was while praying to him that I realized I could make Oinari-sama's shrine my home as well. There was room enough underneath the building for me to sleep. It was easy to remove two boards in the rear of the shrine. I climbed in through the hole. The floor of the shrine above me was so high that I could easily sit up. It was an ideal little house for someone my size, and if I kept quiet no one would discover that I was there. I collected armfuls of dried grass and leaves to spread as bedding. That night the Oinari-sama shrine kept night and the distant stars away and I slept well. Once, hearing something move just outside the wooden wall, I awoke. I thought it might be Oinari-sama. It did not frighten me, for I felt that the fox god would do me no harm.

For many weeks I had searched for Aya-san and little Matsu, hoping in some miraculous way to find them again. Part of me knew that they had died, yet another part of me denied it. I wanted to will them back to life so that I would be less lonely. By fall I finally gave up all hope. Yet sometimes when I saw a woman and child far away, my heart would beat faster and I would think, "That is Aya-san." I met Aya-san's husband, the charcoal hawker, but he did not want to know me. He was standing by a woman who was roasting and selling chestnuts. She was doing good business, for there was a chill in the air. Aya-san's husband had bought some and was peeling and eating them. I pulled at his jacket to attract his attention. He looked at me and sniffed as if he had smelled something unpleasant.

"It is me, Saru," I said and looked expectantly up at him, hoping at least to get some chestnuts.

"Saru," he repeated, shaking his head as he ate the last of his chestnuts. "I have never known anyone named Saru."

"I lived with Aya-san," I said incredulously. "My father paid her to take care of me. You are the one who named me Saru."

"Very fitting. Do you have a tail?" He turned me around to look. "I thought all monkeys had tails." He winked at the woman selling the chestnuts and ordered another batch.

"You are Aya-san's husband!" I declared angrily.

"Aya-san. I don't know any Aya-san." He popped another chestnut into his mouth, flicked the shells in my face, then turned his back on me. As I walked away I looked back. He had turned, too, and was grinning. I made a face at him, and that night I prayed to Oinari-sama that he would starve to death.

I grew not in wisdom but in cunning and learned to trust no one but myself. I became like one of those stray cats that comes to feed at your house but will not allow you to touch it. I considered the whole world my enemy and was suspicious of anyone who treated me kindly. Yet I depended on others to keep alive. I began to understand the maxims of the outcasts and make them my own: that fools were contemptible and created for the "wise," like myself, to cheat. That a soft heart implied a head not much harder. That the rules of law are made to be broken by those outside them and that someone like myself need not bother to think too deeply about how he obtained the food that filled his belly.

By the time of the first snowfall, which came some weeks before the new year, I was fairly snug inside the little shrine. I do not mean that I did not freeze—I did, but I had some rags to cover me and some old rice bags to lie upon. Now that it was winter, the nights were terribly long and I longed for company. Sometimes when I could not sleep I would tell myself stories, but they were always sad. Sometimes I would just lie and cry myself to sleep. I had to be careful, for if anyone approached the little shrine I had to be still. If I was discovered I would certainly be thrown out of Oinari-sama's tiny house of worship.

Not many people came to pray to my little god, and those who came were either old and poor or the very young. Most came to ask for money or rice. "Please give me one coin of silver, and I shall give you some sake each day for a month." Sometimes they would start arguing with Oinari-sama as if he had answered them and told them they were asking too much. "Please, Oinari-sama, ten copper coins, then?" When the little god did not answer, they might in desperation lower their demands to one mon, telling the fox of a sick child who needed medicine. It was hard to keep perfectly still, and I hardly dared breathe while someone was there. Several times I felt like answering for Oinari-sama. I even imagined what kind of a voice the god would have: very high, just like the wind.

Once I did not speak but laughed. I simply could not help it. It was a woman of middle age, or maybe younger, for then I considered anyone above twenty middle-aged. She had come several times to the shrine and often brought some fried bean curd, which I used to eat as soon as she had gone. Once it was still lukewarm. She held long conversations with Oinari-sama, telling him all her troubles and asking his advice. Once she had stated a question, she paused for Oinari-sama to answer; then, as the god remained silent, she answered herself. Her greatest problem was that she was poor and that her husband was fond of squandering his money in sake shops.

"But what should I do, Oinari-sama? . . . That is right, he is my husband, and at my age you cannot get another. I have always been an obedient wife and brought him two children, both sons. . . . That is true, they are good children, but they eat . . . that is only natural, for children grow. The keeper of the sake shop is fat. She grows sideways each year. Soon she will need a larger sliding door to get in and out. She grows fat from money that should have gone to my children, is that not so? . . . Yes, that is true, and she is very ugly, too. Oinari-sama, I have heard that sometimes a fox can get into a woman and make her mad. If you knew a fox that might be willing, Oinari-sama, I would give you bean curd for a whole year."

Suddenly the woman broke off in the middle of a further appeal for Oinari-sama to possess the fat innkeeper and make her mad and started to pray to Buddha. "Namu Amida Butsu, namu Amida Butsu," she droned on and on. At this I could not help laughing, and the poor woman screamed and fled as if three hundred devils were after her. She never came back to the shrine. If Oinari-sama did not miss her, I did—for there was no more fried bean curd for me.

3 *A Long, Cold Winter*

Shortly after the New Year there was a heavy snowfall, and my bare feet were the color of the sky from trudging through it. The snow stayed on the ground for a long time, and Mount Fuji was covered in snow. The days were brilliantly clear, and at night the stars were very bright. The priest in the little temple felt sorry for me and gave me hot food once a day and a pair of straw sandals, but my feet were still numb most of the time. If they did get warm, they hurt and burned as if they were on fire. I found a little companion in my misery: a half-grown cat almost as hungry as I was. I fed him, and he slept in my "house," giving and receiving warmth from me. Two miserable little strays.

I did not give him a name, just called him "Neko," or "cat." He was striped and had green eyes. When the shrine got warm, he purred with pleasure. Through the night when I could not sleep I used to talk to him. I told him about Aya-san and Matsu. This was silly, for surely a cat cannot understand our language, but he made me feel less lonely. I took good care of him as if that chore somehow made up for the fact that no one took care of me. I was in a way both the cat's keeper and the cat. Poor little Neko, cold and hungry most of the time; poor little Saru, his master, just as cold and hungry.

I would wander far afield from my little shrine since it was too cold to stay still. I often carried Neko on my wanderings, keeping him inside my clothes so that he stayed warm. My clothes? My rags would be a more fitting description. Innermost I had what once had been a part of a summer kimono cut down to my size two years before by Aya-san. Who had worn it before me I did not know. My outer garment was an old hunting jacket, once well padded, but sadly in need of repair. This, besides a loincloth, was my whole costume. The hunting jacket had once belonged to Aya-san's husband. It was naturally much too large for me, though this was an advantage as it reached to my knees. Whether I was dirtier than my clothes, or my clothes dirtier than me, I cannot say. But filthy I must have been. I washed my face with the snow each morning and rubbed my feet until they were warm at night.

It was the second month of the new year, and you could feel that the sun was gaining strength. Still the earth was covered in snow, though it was melting now and the sound of flowing water could be heard. I had gone far from my home and was near Tsutsujigasaki Castle. Takeda Katsuyori was collecting an army, and messages had been sent to every district in Kai for all Samurais and their attendants to come to Kofuchu. Many had already obeyed his command, and great crowds had gathered everywhere. There were people selling everything from roasted yams and chestnuts to lucky charms which would deliver whoever wore them from the arrows of his enemies.

I was watching a tumbler on a straw mat who was showing his skill, hoping to gain some coppers. Neko had stuck his head out and was watching, too. Suddenly, not impressed by the agility of the acrobat, he jumped out and ran. I ran after him, but because of the crowd I lost sight of him. When I found him again he, too, had become part of a performance watched by the crowd. A group of boys some years older than I, splendidly dressed and carrying bows and arrows, were getting ready to shoot poor Neko. One boy, obviously more important than the others, told them to stop, claiming that the cat was his to shoot. Neko had jumped into a small tree and was sitting in a cleft between two branches. The boy had bent his bow and was sighting along his arrow. Many grownups were watching and shouting encouragement to him.

I did not hesitate but ran to the cat. I could easily pull him down from the tree with one hand while I stroked him with the other.

"Leave the cat alone," the boy shouted furiously.

"He is mine," I said, standing and looking at him. I had never seen anyone so finely dressed.

"If I can't shoot the cat then I will shoot you!" the boy declared and lifted his bow again. "Stand still!" he ordered.

I do not know why I obeyed. I watched him almost as if I were a mere spectator, not the target. I kept stroking Neko, and he purred with pleasure. For a while the boy and I stood staring at each other; then, just as I was thinking, "Now he is going to shoot," he lowered the bow.

"If you had tried to run I would have shot you," he said and let the arrow fly. It stuck in the ground near my foot.

I reached down, drew it out, walked over to the boy, and handed it to him. He took it and returned it to its quiver with a laugh. Everyone who had been watching laughed, too. I stuffed Neko inside my clothes and walked away.

Had I been scared? I thought about it all the way back to my little shrine. Not really, I decided, yet I felt sure that what the boy had said was true: if I had tried to run he would have shot me. Who was he? Some high-ranking Samurai's son or maybe a Takeda. It didn't matter, not to me!

"He would have shot you, Neko," I whispered to the cat as I got down. "Oinari-sama, give him a stomachache tonight," I prayed, looking up at the little stone figures of the foxes which flanked the tiny shrine.

That night I dreamed again about my father. He came all dressed like a very important person, but when he saw me he said, "No, that is not my son—he is too dirty." I felt very ashamed. Suddenly, the boy with the bow and arrow appeared, and my father said that he was his son. Then I woke. I felt wretched because of the dream, but the sun was already up and the sky was cloudless. "You have no father and no mother, so stop dreaming about them," I admonished myself. At that moment Neko got up and started to rub himself against my face. He was hungry. "You are my little brother," I said and grinned. "Maybe you are Oinari-sama? If a fox can change itself into a human being maybe it can change itself into a cat as well." This made me laugh as I climbed out of my "house." The evening before I had heard someone come to pray at the shrine. Maybe they had left something? I was in luck—bean curd. I broke a piece off it and gave it to Neko, who ate quickly and looked up at me as if to say, "I want more." "We share," I said and gave him some more, then ate the rest myself. Two pieces of tofu are not enough when you are hungry. It only increases your hunger.

A few days later it started to rain, and the streets and pathways turned into mud. Like most beggars, I had a certain number of "patrons." First among them was the priest at the temple, but there were others, too, or I should probably have starved to death. One was a woman who had a soba shop. Her noodles were delicious, and sometimes she would give me a bowlful. If I were especially lucky she would have a guest who would give me a copper coin as well. I do not think that her noodles were better than those served at other places—the same buckwheat flour had been used—but she was always cheerful. Her face was round like the full moon and her eyes so small that they almost disappeared when she smiled. Haru-san was shaped more like a koku of rice than a willow tree—graceful she was not. Somehow she made her customers feel that life was not altogether a path in darkness. Her soba shop consisted of one room and a small kitchen where she cooked. I was allowed to sit in the corner by the door to eat the portion she gave me. Because I looked so wet that day, she gave me a larger amount than usual. A poor Samurai from somewhere in the mountains was enjoying his soba and drinking sake. When he saw me he thought it time for some good-natured fun.

"Are you feeding the rats of the town, Oharu?" he asked.

"Only the ones who have cats along," Haru-san answered and laughed.

The Samurai then noticed Neko, whose head stuck out from my clothes.

"Will you sell me your cat and I will have it roasted for dinner?" he asked, looking at me and winking at Haru-san. She entered into the spirit of the joke to please her customer and replied that the cat was too skinny to roast but she thought she could stew it. I do not know why I believed they were seriously discussing poor Neko as a dish. Frantically, I said I would not sell my cat. This sent the Samurai into gales of laughter. He held up a silver coin and offered it to me. I had never seen a silver coin, so I stared at it. The Samurai was probably a little scared that I would agree, for he was a poor man himself, and he tucked it away. Still grinning, he said that maybe the boy would make a better dish. It was then I realized they had only been jesting. Quickly, I put out my hand and begged. It was a good moment. I could see that the man did not want to give me anything, but in front of Haru-san he was ashamed to show himself as mean. Grudgingly, he took a copper mon from his purse and handed it to me. I bowed low, thanked him three times, and slipped out of the kitchen.

It had stopped raining, and strolling along I felt very satisfied with myself. I had money. Though the copper mon would not buy me much, it made me feel very rich. I wandered into an area where there were many sake shops. I watched a Samurai, too wealthy and finely dressed to enter any of the humble drinking places. A man dressed in beggar's clothes, not much better than my own, cast himself on the ground in front of the noble Samurai. He was kneeling in a puddle of water, and as he knocked his head on the ground he made little ripples in it. The Samurai looked at him with great contempt. The beggar said something I could not hear. The Samurai lifted one foot and sent the supplicant sprawling. As the Samurai walked away, the beggar made a gesture of contempt toward his back. Getting to his feet he spied me, ran over, and hit me as hard as he could, as punishment for having witnessed his shame. I fell to the ground, and the man spat at me before walking away. I did not understand why he had done this and cried loudly like the child I was. I have never forgotten it. I can still remember looking up into his face and seeing the hatred there.

4 *Spring Finally Comes*

For those who are so wealthy that they can afford to waste charcoal to keep themselves warm, winter holds few fears. They also have clothes which are heavily lined so that the sharp winds which blow at the end of the year cannot penetrate them. They may even find the snow-laden branches of the trees lovelier than when they are covered with flowers. But to the poor, the desperate, winter is like a sentence passed on a criminal. So many weeks, so many months, before the sun once more will have the power to tempt the buds of the trees to open and entice the flowers to unfold and bloom.

The second month of the year passed, and still the sky was dark and the river all ice. Old people died by the score, and children were found frozen to death. I do not know how I survived, but I remember how long a night can be when you are too cold to sleep. I would lie curled up rubbing one foot against the other to try and keep warm, wondering if I would be alive when the sun rose.

Suddenly, one morning spring finally came! I woke and I wasn't cold. "The winter is over," I said to Neko and stroked him. He purred as if he had understood what I had said. "Soon it will be really warm and I shall get a fishhook and catch you a fat fish in the river," I said and smiled.

The poor are like animals in that they live from day to day —there is no point in dreaming about tomorrow. Maybe because of this they enjoy more intensely the smaller pleasures of life. As I felt the warmth of the sun penetrating my body and warming my bones, I almost purred like Neko. With my bowl in hand I went to the temple nearby to beg some gruel for breakfast.

"Saru, spring has come!" The priest smiled at me. "Soon the plum trees will blossom." He led me to the kitchen and gave me a bowl, not of gruel, but of rice. Then he poured two cups of tea and handed one of them to me. "May Katsuyori be victorious!" he said in a solemn tone of voice. I looked at him in surprise, for I knew that no one thought that Takeda Katsuyori would succeed. "If only Yoshinobu had not killed himself," he added. Takeda Yoshinobu had been forced by his father, Shingen, to commit suicide, seppuku. Now, because everyone was dissatisfied with his half brother, Katsuyori, they all felt sorry that he had died. Yoshinobu had plotted against his father, wanting to overthrow him and take his place as chief of the Takedas. I thought for a moment of the boy who had aimed his arrow at me and Neko and wondered if he could have been Katsuyori's son. "If only his father had not died, he might now have been ruler of all Japan and Kofuchu its capital." I had heard this dream, or wish, before so it did not surprise me. I always agreed to whatever was said by my "patrons," and I was willing to accept the most foolish statement as words of wisdom. Now I mumbled assent as if he had expressed exactly my opinion. I was very happy because I was warm and no longer hungry.

"Soon we will have to fight," the priest said, and I was reminded of the people who came to worship at Oinari-sama's little temple. He was agreeing with himself. "We might be able to win against Tokugawa Iyeyasu." Since the priest was discussing weighty matters he had a very serious expression. "But against both Oda Nobunaga and Iyeyasu, we could never win." Suddenly the priest looked at me cunningly as if he had suddenly gotten a clever idea. "Now, Saru, if we could only get Uesugi Kenshin on our side all could be well." Uesugi Kenshin was the lord of the neighboring province Echigo and a mighty warrior who had fought Takeda Shingen many times in the past. "I am Neko," I suddenly thought. "He is talking to himself rather than to me. Just as I talk to my cat when I am alone, and probably I understood no more of the politics of our province of Kai or the whole country than poor Neko." I felt that it was time I said something, though I had nodded a few times to show I was listening.

"When do you think the battle will take place?" I asked knowingly.

"Late in the spring or sometime this summer. Katsuyori is brave like his father, but he is not as wise as he was."

"My father died in the battle of Mikata-ga-hara," I said, and I had said this so many times that the words had lost all meaning to me. Whenever I went begging I would always start my demand by droning those words, but so did every beggar child, even if his father was still alive.

"I know, Saru." The priest nodded to show that he approved of the time and place my father had chosen for this death. I looked down at my empty bowl; the priest smiled, took it, and scooped another spoonful of rice into it.

The weather held and the priest's promise that the plum trees would soon blossom came true. With the warmth the soldiers that Takeda Katsuyori had sent for started to arrive. Bushis came from all over Kai with their servants and foot soldiers. Soon the population of Kofuchu had more than doubled, and at night there was not an empty space in any of the houses, temples, or shrines large enough for a cat to curl up in. The fields around the town were filled with horses for which, because of the hard winter we had had, it was difficult to find fodder. The owners of sake shops did good business, and at night the streets were filled with vendors cooking and selling food.

With the soldiers came beggars and men and women who thought to make their fortune among those gathered here. I had to be more careful about my home, for there were many more who came to worship at the Oinari-sama little shrine. This meant that more bean curd or rice balls were left but also that I might be discovered. In front of the shrine was an iron box for worshippers to drop money in. Once in a while it was emptied by someone from a Shinto shrine; he was not a priest, I think he was just a caretaker. I suspect that he knew I slept underneath Oinari-sama's little house, but he had decided to do nothing about it. Once when I met him he grinned in a knowing way.

One day I was watching some boy tumblers performing in

the street. The youngest was about my age. It was as if they had no bones in their bodies because they could twist this way and that. One who was walking around on his hands had bent his back so completely that his head was sticking out between his legs, which, in turn, stuck up in the air as if they had decided to become hands. I shuddered as I looked at him. He looked so misshapen that I finally turned away in order not to see him.

"They train them when they are very small, before they can even walk. I have been told that they hang them up by the hands and put weights on their feet in order to stretch them." A man behind me was speaking. He had been watching the young acrobats, too.

"That must hurt. I like it much better when they just turn somersaults," I said, looking at him. He was leaning on a cleft stick, which supported him under the arm. One of his legs was hanging uselessly, not touching the ground.

"I got a gash at Mikata-ga-hara, and ever since it has been like that," he explained, noticing that I had been looking at his crippled leg. "The wound healed, but my leg is like a disobedient child—it won't listen to what I say and does not obey me." He grinned and said that he now was three-legged, counting his stick as his third leg.

"My father died at Mikata-ga-hara," I said, wondering if what he had told me was the truth. "He is a beggar," I thought, "and a beggar's word cannot be trusted."

"What troops did he belong to?" the cripple asked. When I answered Lord Naito's, he claimed that he had served Lord Naito, too, and wanted to know my father's name.

"My foster mother—for my real mother died when I was born—said his name was Kasuke."

"Did he carry a spear or was he a bowman? I knew someone by that name. Was he big and broadly built and carried a spear?"

"I don't know," I answered, feeling ashamed. "I cannot remember him. I was not much more than a baby when he left." The last time my father had come to see me—and to pay Aya-san—I had been just a little over two years old. To such a tiny one, all grownups were giants. It pleased me to hear that he had been "big and broadly built."

"We were on the left flank, in the very forefront of battle."

"He died facing the enemy." I uttered the foolish phrase I often used when begging. It made the stranger laugh.

"Whether he got an arrow through his chest or his back is all the same to him now . . . yes, Kasuke, that was his name, he told me once he had a son in Kofuchu."

"What was he like?" I asked eagerly.

"He was a man, a soldier like the rest of us. In the winter he tried to keep warm and in the summer cool. He liked his food and some sake when he could get it." Seeing the disappointment mirrored in my face he added, "He was no worse than the rest of us and better than most. You need not feel ashamed of him. Though he won't be reborn a Buddha, he won't be a fly either."

The acrobats had finished, and now they were passing among the spectators, begging. Some people who had watched turned shamefacedly away, but others sneered at the tumblers and few gave them anything. To my surprise the cripple I had been talking to took a coin from inside his rags and threw it to the youngest of them. Seeing my astonishment, he fished out another copper mon and gave it to me.

"Thank you," I said and twice bowed deeply.

"Come with me!" he commanded and began to hobble away. For a moment I hesitated, but then, because he had known my father and maybe even more because he had given me a coin, I followed.

5 *A Gang of Thieves*

The man set off toward the river. I carefully kept a few paces behind him. I did not know why I didn't trust him. Once he turned to see if I was following. He smiled and made a motion with his free hand; then he hobbled on, his other hand clutching the stick he was leaning on. I drew a little nearer but still refrained from walking beside him. He could take this as humility on my part if he wanted to.

In a very mean part of the town he finally stopped in front of a hovel. The house had a bit of land around it, which was probably why it had been spared during the great fire the year before. It was old, but even when it had been built it had not been much more than a large shack. A very tall tree grew in front of it, and there were some bushes, too, which half hid it. The thatched roof was very weatherworn, and I doubted that it would keep out the rain for many more years.

"My castle," he said with a grin. I nodded and smiled. He waited for me to go in in front of him, but I hung back. Finally, with a shrug of his shoulders, he walked up the tiny path leading to the house and I followed. With great difficulty he climbed up to a narrow open portico. He paused as if to say something, then thought better of it and opened the door.

"You need not be afraid," he said, holding the door.

"I am not." I lied, for I was, if not afraid, at least apprehensive.

The house had only one large room. In the corner was a ladder leading to a loft. It seemed to have been built for storage rather than for living. A group of youngsters, somewhat older than myself, greeted us. They were sitting on the rough wooden floor, drinking tea. As we entered they bowed toward my companion but did not get up. Throwing away his stick, he ordered tea and collapsed rather than sat down on the floor. One of the boys brought him a pillow and helped to push it under him when he lifted himself by his hands. He looked around, his glance dwelling for a moment on the faces of each of the five boys, then, turning to me, he said, "I forgot to ask you your name."

"I have none," I said and blushed. "But people call me Saru."

The cripple laughed. "Iwa-saru, I presume, for you are not too fond of talking."

I knew what he was referring to: the three monkeys, one who hides his eyes, the second who holds his ears, and the third, Iwa-saru, who holds a paw in front of his mouth. Hear no evil, see no evil, and speak no evil. It was true that if I was one of the three, it was Iwa-saru and certainly not Kika-saru, who is pictured putting his paws on his ears in order not to hear. I liked to hear and to see, too, but talking could often get you into trouble. Instinctively, I felt that it was wise not to waste one's breath.

"I knew Saru's father. We were at Mikata-ga-hara together." The cripple looked at the boys as if expecting them to object to what he had just said. "He died there," he added.

At that moment I thought, "He is lying; he never knew my father, and he was never at Mikata-ga-hara." I tried to recall if he had said anything which might prove that he was speaking the truth and had known my father. I couldn't. It was I who had said that my father had been one of Lord Naito's men and told him his name. Why had he lied, and what did he want with me? I wondered and was on my guard.

Looking at me, much as if he was inspecting a horse, the oldest of the boys said, "He is too young."

"He is agile, I think, and clever, Nezumi," responded the cripple.

The boy called Nezumi, which means rat, scrutinized me once more but came to the same conclusion, for he shook his head.

"They are a gang of robbers," I thought, glancing at the one who was nearest to my age. He looked back at me and made a face. I did not object to stealing—I had stolen myself, otherwise I would have been dead, but I did not think I wanted to join such a gang. In a strange way, having managed to live through the winter, I had come to prize my independence. Here I would be the servant of all. Then if they were caught, their heads would be put on stakes in the field of execution and one might die because of someone else's mistake or foolishness. A few days before, Katsuyori had put to death some of the hostages he held, the wife and the brother of a Samurai who had gone over to his enemies. She had been strangled; I had seen her severed head displayed on a stake. Next to hers had been the heads of some bandits, one of them belonging to a boy no older than myself. I did not want to end my life before it had begun and had no confidence that these little thieves and their master would escape their fate.

"He is alone, no parents, no family." The cripple spoke hurriedly, and I thought I saw him wink. "He is so young that no one will notice him, or what is important, suspect him."

Nezumi shook his head once more, looked me over again, then said: "You should not have brought him, now he can tell."

I wanted to protest that I wouldn't tell anyone anything, but then I decided that that would probably arouse their suspicions.

"How old are you, child?" he asked contemptuously.

"I was born in Eiroku ten." I gave the name of the nengo, the name given by the emperor to that period when I was born, rather than actually telling my age. The nengo had been changed twice since I was born, and now it was the second year of Tensho. Sometimes the emperor would change the nengo several times during his reign, which confused everyone and made it difficult, especially for the very old, to figure out their ages. Ogimachi-tenno had changed the nengo three times since he had become emperor. Just as I expected, my answer confused the boy. It was hard for me not to smile. But you must never smile at anyone unless you know him and he is your friend, or your enemy to whom you have decided to show your true feeling. Your face should always be as still as a winter landscape, I was once told by the priest at the temple. It is often the expression on a man's face rather than words spoken that gets him into trouble.

"Which means that you are five." Deliberately Nezumi guessed too young, hoping to make me call out my actual age. For a moment I hesitated.

"If you say so." I bowed my head submissively and carefully lowered my gaze.

"He is seven," the cripple said irritatedly. "Nengo Eiroku ten was seven years ago."

"So why could he not say that?" Nezumi looked darkly at me. "You should not have brought him," he repeated.

It is funny that when I sense danger my back grows cold. Even in the warmest of summers it is as if a cold wind suddenly touches it. I felt this now. The last time I had felt it had been when the young boy with the bow had sighted his arrow at me. "They don't trust me," I thought. "They are scared that I will tell where they live." I said nothing, for I knew if I pleaded that I would tell no one I would never leave the house alive.

"Where do you live, child?" Nezumi looked down at the floor as if my answer was of no importance to him.

I gave the name of the temple where the priest sometimes fed me, not of Oinari-sama's little shrine.

"The priest allows you to stay there?" I could tell that he did not believe me. I looked at the cripple and answered as if it were he and not the boy who had asked me.

"I sweep the place and run errands for him." I tried to keep even the tiniest vestige of fear out of my voice. "I have stayed there all winter."

Suddenly one of the other boys said, "I have seen him there, I think it is true."

I looked at the boy in surprise. He carefully kept his glance from me. He must have been twelve or maybe even more.

Nezumi, older and the leader of the others, got up. He walked over to me slowly, yet as agile as a cat ready to pounce. His legs astride, he stood looking down at me. I met his glance. Suddenly he drew a knife and pressed the point of the weapon against my throat so lightly that it did not break the skin. "You have never been here," he said.

"No," I whispered and then repeated his words: "I have never been here."

He pressed the knife a little. I could feel the pain as it broke the skin, but I did not move.

"Oh, let him be." The boy who claimed to have seen me at the temple stood up. My tormentor looked at him and then down at me. He withdrew the knife and hid it among his clothes again. "I wanted him to know what will happen to him if he tells anyone—even the priest—about where he has been."

"He has been warned, so let him go." The two boys glared at each other, and for a moment I thought they would fight. They would have been evenly matched, for although the boy called Nezumi was older, the younger boy looked stronger. Then suddenly their leader shrugged his shoulders as if to say, "What do I care?" and, pointing to the door, told me to get out.

Turning to the cripple and then to the boys, I bowed twice and walked to the door. As I closed it behind me, I wanted desperately to run, but did not do so until I was out of sight of the house. I stopped for a moment and touched my neck. I looked at my hand. There was a little spot of blood on it. I wiped it on my sleeve and then ran as fast as I could. I did not stop until I came to my home, the little shrine of Oinari-sama. Neko was lying in the sun. I picked him up, and he purred and started to lick my neck. I laughed and said to the cat, "He would have killed me, I am sure of it."

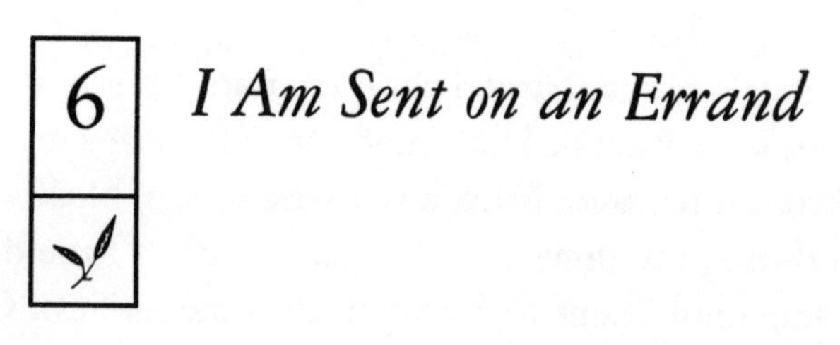

6 I Am Sent on an Errand

"Did you see them leave, Saru?" the priest asked eagerly. "It was a wonderful sight! How can anyone beat an army like that?"

I nodded, as usual, agreeing to anything the priest said. Lord Takeda Katsuyori had left with the greater part of his army. I had watched and had even seen Lord Naito riding past. I thought he looked very haughty. Once I had taken courage to go to his house to beg and told his servant that my father had been one of Lord Naito's soldiers. The servant had laughed and claimed that any little beggar child could say that. Then he had told me to clear out or he would kick me out, and watched me until I was outside the gate of the compound. That morning, looking at the soldiers, I imagined that one of them was my father. I tried to choose one of them. Not one of the grand lords, or the mounted ones, no, one of the ordinary foot soldiers. The kind who, when they die in battle, keep their heads, as they are not important enough to be cut off as trophies. I finally settled on a funny little man with a limp who carried a lance. He looked clever, as if he might survive a battle.

"The Kai cavalry is famous all over Japan." The priest had a habit of saying such things as if he were disclosing important information. "There is no braver soldier than a Kai Bushi." The priest looked as proud as if he were one himself. "I am sure that both Nobunaga and Iyeyasu are worried today." The priest uttered the names of these famous warlords as if he knew them personally.

"Where are they going?" I asked. I had been given food, but I was hoping to be offered tea.

"Toward Tokugawa Iyeyasu's castle in Mikawa, I would guess. Did you see our Lord Takeda Katsuyori?"

I nodded.

"He is not his father, but then how could he be?" The priest sighed as if this made him sad. Then, more cheerfully, he said, "But he is as brave as his father."

I made a sound of agreement and looked away to hide a smile. Last night, I had heard some soldiers discussing their lord. None seemed to have much liking for him, and one had called him a fool.

"Saru, you are a clever little monkey." The priest looked affectionately at me. "Are you still hungry? Would you like some tea?"

I bowed my head deeply to signify both that I would like some tea and that I was very grateful. I was wondering if the cripple or one of the boys from the gang of robbers had been around to find out if I had told the truth when I said I lived at the temple. I did not dare ask.

The priest brought me not only a cup of tea but a bean-paste sweet, too. I knew that most people had little respect for him. He was too good-natured and too easy to take advantage of. Even most beggars respect those whose hearts are stones.

"You are a strange child, Saru." The priest watched me eat the bean-paste sweet. "Sometimes I think you are not a child at all but maybe some kind of mountain sprite that has taken on human shape."

"I am not a Tengu." I smiled, for my nose is very short, and the Tengu, the goblin that lives in the mountains, has a very long nose. Then, for he was so kind to me, I said, "But you are right, maybe I am not a child. Maybe when you have never known a father or a mother, then you can't be a child." I had never thought about it before, but suddenly I realized that I had never played. I had watched other children play, but I could not recall ever having done so myself. I did not feel sad or sorry because of this. It was my fate, and if I wanted to survive I could not be a child. I put down my cup and rose.

Twice I bowed deeply.

"You can come every day," the priest said. "There will always be something here for you, Saru."

"Thank you very much." Once more I bowed. He was kind, and I was very grateful to him. I doubt if I would have lived through that winter without his help.

As I walked through the town I thought of myself almost as if I were another person. "You are clever," I thought, "but I am not sure that that is not the best that can be said. You are not really kind, not that that matters, but are you brave?" I thought for a moment before answering myself. "I don't think I am, but then my father's bravery only earned him an arrow through his chest." That time with the boys, I had been frightened. I knew that their leader would have liked to kill me. Not so much because he was scared that I would tell someone about him and his gang. No, he wanted to do it for an entirely different reason. It had to do with his followers and with the cripple. He needed to show who was master and, by killing me, he felt he would have proved it.

The town which had been so overcrowded that morning now felt strangely empty. Most of the street hawkers had left with the army. I still had the coin the cripple had given me; now I spent it buying a dish of steaming noodles. I had not really been hungry, but I could always eat and the smell of the noodles cooking had tempted me. An old Samurai walked by, too old to fight anymore except in his dreams. He looked at me for a moment. I thought of holding out my hand but decided against it. He would not have given me anything even if I had gone down on my knees. You cannot be too humble when you beg from a Bushi. It is best to kneel and let your forehead touch the ground. If the Samurai deigns to give you a coin he will throw it on the ground, never hand it to you. I hated the Samurais, the Bushis, and I seldom begged from them. When I did I always told them about my father, whereas when I begged from a woman I would tell how my mother had died giving birth to me. I smiled at the thought of my inheritance, a dead mother and father, both very useful for a beggar. The old Samurai frowned haughtily and suddenly walked over to me.

"Boy," he said, and I fell to my knees, "I want someone to run an errand for me."

I bowed to show that I was willing but said nothing, only looking up at him expectantly.

"There is a woman who has an inn east of here down by the river. She is well known. When the river is up, her son ferries people across. Her husband was once my servant. He is dead now." For a moment the old man paused, as if, in his mind, conjuring up a picture of his dead servant. "I want her son to come to me as soon as he can."

"Sir, is she an old woman with a scar on her cheek? Her name, I think, is Sumi-san," I said.

"That is right." The old Bushi smiled. "What is your name?" he asked.

"People call me Saru, sir."

"And are you one?" The old man grinned.

"If you think I am, then I am a monkey. My father was a soldier and was killed at Mikata-ga-hara."

"And your mother?"

"She died when I was born, sir."

"Mother and fatherless—there will be more of your kind soon—I think you are a monkey. Do you know who I am?"

I shook my head and whispered, "No, My Lord."

"Akiyama Nobutora. When you have delivered my message I shall reward you." Lord Akiyama turned away. I knew his son had been one of Takeda Shingen's generals, and his mansion was not far from the castle. I stayed kneeling on the ground until he had gone. Then I jumped up, eager to be gone. It would take me at least a couple of hours to get to the inn even if I walked fast. "A reward," I thought. "That must be more than a few copper mons. A silver coin at least." As I ran I imagined the fortune which might be mine.

I did not like the Samurais, the Bushis, but that did not mean that I did not value any connection with them. They were the rulers and the rest of us the ruled. Lord Akiyama was not just a Bushi, no, he was a lord, a man who owned land which gave him an income—maybe several thousand kokus of rice. He was great enough to sit in the council of Takeda Katsuyori, the lord of our province of Kai.

I ran the first ri, but by then I was tired and sat down to rest under a tree. I had at least another ri to go before I would be at the inn. It was a warm spring day, and the tree I rested under was a plum tree in full flower. Already some of the petals were falling on the ground like fresh snow. For the poor, spring is the best time of the year because winter is so far away that there is no point in worrying about it. You can hope and dream that the summer will bring you something pleasant. When you go to the temples or the shrines to pray, there is less despair in your prayers than in those you offered the gods in winter. In winter you pray to survive. In the spring you are more ambitious. Then you dare make demands of the gods, asking for gifts rather than begging to be allowed to live. I noticed that near me was a stone Jizo statue. It was very poorly carved and stood a little crookedly as if the Jizo was tired. Like Oinari-sama, the Jizos are prayed to by simple people, poor people who feel ashamed when visiting a temple. There they only mumble so low that the god probably won't hear them. But to the local Jizo statue, they dare talk about their personal problems. Here there is no need for formality. The great Amida Buddha is perfection. The local Jizo is no nearer perfection than the people who pray to him. He understands hunger and cold. After all, he is not housed in a temple but must brave the weather beside the road where he has been put. He is one of them. He belongs to the village. He knows them all and is there to protect and help them. As I got up, I stopped for a minute in front of the statue. "Jizo-bosatsu," I said, "I am a very poor boy who has neither a father nor a mother. Please protect and help me." Then I bowed twice and walked on.

A little while later my road was crossed by a path leading to a small village. I could see a group of houses. Here there were three Jizo statues, but I noticed only the man resting in front of them. His stick was leaning up against one of the stone figures. It was the cripple.

"So, Saru, we meet again," he said.

"Yes," I admitted and bowed, but not very low.

"Where are you going?" As I did not answer, he asked sarcastically, "Have you come into the country to do some flower viewing?"

"Yes," I mumbled.

"Like the rich who have little else to do but to sit under flowering cherry trees and compose poems, Saru has come flower viewing. But I see you carry neither brush nor paper to write on."

"I can't write," I admitted reluctantly.

"That is a pity, but then most monkeys can't. Maybe I will come with you. We can go flower viewing together."

"No," escaped me, for I did not want to have anything to do with the man. I felt he was dangerous, that he had some strange sickness I could catch.

"If we had ink and an ink stone and brush and paper I could write your poems down for you." The cripple grinned. "But maybe you are in a hurry?"

"Yes," I agreed and turned to walk away.

"Remember, Saru," the cripple called after me, "that monkeys, too, can fall from trees."

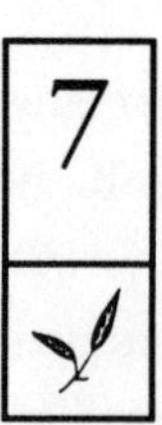

7 *The Crippled Thief Again*

I took the cripple's words for what they were: not only a warning but a threat. Monkeys are agile, adept at climbing, but, in spite of this, they, too, can fall from trees. What he meant was: next time you won't escape as you did last time we met. "I must be careful," I thought, for both the cripple and the leader of the gang disliked me now. Without wishing to, I had become involved in their lives. I had seen the cripple, a grown man, humiliated by a youngster who could have been his son. Then I had been used by one of the boys as the pretext for a revolt, and he, the leader, had had to let me go. I wondered what had happened later in that strange old house. I doubted if the two boys had fought. But I was sure that the leader of the gang had not forgotten the incident or that I was the cause of it. If he could not revenge himself on the younger boy, he could upon me if he ever met up with me again. "I am Iwa-saru, the silent monkey. I shall keep my eyes open," I muttered.

I knew of the inn and the woman who ran it, although I had never actually been there. It had a strange reputation, and so did its owner. It was said that she was in touch with spirits, ghosts that haunted her place. Some said that she was not a woman at all but a fox who had taken on human shape. Aya-san's husband, the charcoal seller, had spoken of her. Her inn was not so much a foxes' den as a den of thieves. I was eager to see it for myself. Sleeping under the Oinari-sama little shrine had made me unafraid of ghosts and goblins. I had spent too many long nights in darkness to fear them. The sounds you hear at night can as readily be explained as those you hear in the daytime. The fear of darkness is inside yourself, not in the night.

The building was larger than I had expected. It was situated on high ground so that it would not be flooded in spring when the river rose as the snow in the mountains melted. It was old, its wooden walls black with age, and the thatched roof had been patched. I knocked at the door and called out a greeting. No one answered, but a chicken came around the corner of the house as if to see who had come. When no one returned my greeting the third time I shouted it, I slid the door open. Half the entrance hall had an earthen floor, the rest a wooden one. Some straw sandals lay abandoned next to the wooden floor. I entered and closed the door behind me. I took off my own straw sandals and, kneeling on the wooden floor, I put them neatly beside each other on the earthen one. Still kneeling, I listened beside the sliding door, then called out a greeting in a loud voice. There was no answer, but, in spite of the silence, I felt there was someone beyond the door. I slid it back a few inches and looked in. The room was large, but in the dim light I could see no one. Again I sang out my greeting, and from a corner came a grunt in reply. I begged permission to enter, and the voice gave another grunt, which I took for consent. The door squeaked as I slipped it back far enough for me to squeeze through. I closed it carefully and advanced to the middle of the room, where I knelt once more, bowing my head so deeply that it almost touched the floor. I announced why I had come and who had sent me.

"My son has gone. They have taken him away," the voice whined from the corner. As my eyes grew accustomed to the semidarkness of the room, I could see the woman who had spoken.

"Who has taken your son away?" I asked, moving closer to where she sat.

"We belong to Lord Baba. The inn is his. He sent a message for my son to come yesterday, so he has gone."

"I thought your husband served Lord Akiyama."

"He did. My father had the inn here. When he died my husband got permission from our lord to come here, so then he became a retainer of Lord Baba instead. I had only the one son, and now he is gone," she whined, as if he were already dead and she was attending his funeral.

"He will come back," I suggested.

"No!" The old crone shook her head and beckoned me to come closer. On my knees I edged toward her. "Give me your hand!" she demanded. I held it out, and she turned it and peered into my palm. "Everything is written there if you can but read it. You will live to become an old man," she announced and let go of my hand.

"Thank you," I murmured and bowed my head as if I had received a gift.

"Shall I tell the lord that your son has gone with Lord Baba's soldiers and that he is with the army of Katsuyori?" I asked.

"You may tell him whatever you care to. Tell him that . . . he shall lose a son soon, too." Suddenly the old woman started to laugh, but her mirth sounded more like the cawing of a crow than human laughter. "Most of them will die, but not Takeda Katsuyori. A sword will sever his head from his body, but not yet."

"How do you know?" I asked. My question made the old woman laugh once more.

"Old Sumi-san knows—she can tell," she muttered between her cackling.

"She is mad," I thought, "the kind of madness which comes to old people when they live beyond their time." I looked around the room, wondering if I should beg some food or even money. I thought of stealing, too, for if my story is to be true I must not hide anything. I was about to tell my sad story when the woman clapped her hands. The sound made me jump because it was so unexpected.

I heard a door open and looked around. A girl my own age entered.

"What do you want, Grandmother?" she asked and looked at me.

"Give the boy something to eat—he must be hungry. He has walked far."

"I am cooking rice, Grandmother, but it is not ready yet."

"Then take him to the kitchen and let him wait there. He is"—the old woman paused—"a lucky boy. I can tell."

The kitchen was a lean-to attached to the main house. A

large iron pot was hanging over an open fire. I could smell that something good was cooking. I looked at the girl closely while she stared back at me. We were like two dogs sniffing at each other undecided whether to growl or to wag our tails. Abruptly she laughed and said with disdain, "You are dirty."

I felt my face go red. I knew I was dirty, and, because I knew it, I felt doubly ashamed. I looked down at myself. All of a sudden I could see myself as if I were a stranger. "I am very poor," I mumbled, feeling even more wretched.

"Go and wash yourself!" she commanded. As I did not move, she said with pride, "We have a well of our own. Go and wash yourself there." Still I did not move. "Come!" She rose and beckoned me to follow her through a backdoor to a yard. There was a well and not far from it a little bathhouse. She drew a bucket of water from the well and handed it to me. I took the wooden bucket but did not move. "Take your clothes off!" she commanded like a mother to a stupid child.

I took off the charcoal seller's old hunting jacket, revealing the old kimono beneath it. I put the jacket down on the ground, and she poked at it with her toe.

The humiliation drew tears from my eyes. I wiped them with the back of my hand and decided to grab my jacket and run. She spied the tear and felt sorry for me. "I will ask Grandmother for some clothes for you." Sensing my shyness, she pointed to the little hut and said, "You can wash in there."

The bathhouse smelled musty. It had not been used for a long time, and a disagreeable sour smell permeated it. I put the bucket down and felt the water with my hands. It was very cold. I stripped and began washing myself as best as I could. There were some rags hanging on the wall, and I used one of them to scrub myself, thinking I could dry myself with the others. I realized how thin I was. I could feel my own bones. My ribs were plainly visible beneath the skin.

Without warning the door opened. It was the girl. I held the rag in front of me. She carefully acted as if she had not seen me. "Here, my grandmother says you can have these. They belonged to her son when he was a child." She cast a bundle of clothes on the floor and left.

The clothes were a little too large. Besides a kimono there was a boy's quilted jacket—almost new. I looked at the dirty rags which had served to cover me for so long, and touching them with my toes I lifted them off the ground.

"Is that your father who is with Lord Baba's soldiers?" I asked, sitting in the kitchen once more.

"No, that is my uncle. My father is dead, and so is my mother. My father was killed at Mikata-ga-hara. He came from Echigo. He married my mother, who was Grandmother's only daughter."

"When did she die?" I asked rather foolishly, hoping that she, too, had died giving birth, like my mother.

"A few years ago. She was very beautiful."

"My father was killed at Mikata-ga-hara as well. He belonged to Lord Naito's troops. My mother is dead, too."

"Was she very beautiful?" the girl asked.

The question so surprised me that I did not answer immediately. "I don't know," I said. "She died when I was born."

"But was she beautiful like my mother?"

"I have been told she was very young." This was something I had heard Aya-san say. I had never tried to imagine what my mother had looked like, though I had often wondered about my father. "What is your name?" I asked.

"Ume. What is yours?"

"Ume, plum. That is a nice name. I don't have a name, but they call me Saru."

"Why don't you have a name? I thought everyone had one." She dished up a bowlful of rice. It had been cooked with herbs and smelled delicious. "Here!" She handed me a bowl and some chopsticks.

"My father probably gave me a name, but then he died. Aya-san, the woman who took care of me, called me Saru. It was actually her husband who called me that. He sold charcoal, and he knew your grandmother. I heard him talk of her and your inn." I started to eat, and between mouthfuls I told more of my story. How I had lived the winter under Oinari-sama's little shrine and how cold and miserable I had been. I also told her about my cat, Neko. I was not the silent monkey that I usually was. She listened carefully to everything I said, nodding her head to show not so much that she understood but that she sympathized with me in my troubles.

I heard a sound as if someone had come to the inn. A moment later the old lady called for her grandchild. Ume excused herself formally as if I were a grownup and bowed to me before leaving. When she opened the door I could hear someone talking in the next room. I thought I recognized the voice. I slid the door open just enough to see into the room.

The old lady was giving instructions to Ume, who was kneeling in front of her. Next to her sat the cripple, his good leg folded under him. Very carefully I closed the door again. What was he doing here? He was a bird of ill omen.

I picked up my bowl and started to eat the last few grains of rice as I thought about what I should do.

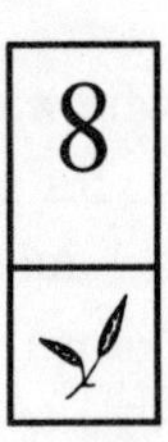

8 *Preparing for Battle*

"Have you ever seen that man before?" I whispered as soon as Ume returned. She looked at me in surprise and shook her head.

"He is a thief, or worse. Don't let him know that I am here." I put my finger in front of my mouth to show that she must not speak loudly.

"He asked to stay and paid Grandmother for a night's lodging, a meal and sake, too," she whispered.

"Come." I rose and beckoned her to follow. We went outside in the yard. I told all I knew about the cripple and the gang of youngsters he belonged to. "I think they plan to rob the inn tonight. He will let them in once you are asleep."

"Will they kill us?" she asked.

"I don't think so." The idea had not even entered my head, but now I considered it. "Yes, maybe they would. I think their leader might like it."

"To kill?" She shook her head as if to get rid of the thought.

"Some people like it, I think." Once I had seen a Samurai

cut the head off a dog that had barked at him. As he lifted his sword the Bushi had a strange expression on his face. At that moment I thought that if it were my head he were cutting off his expression would have been the same.

"But what shall we do?" she wailed. "Oh, if only Uncle were here."

"That is why they have come. Someone has told them that your uncle has left. Do you know of anyone you can ask to help us?" As I spoke I realized that I had inadvertently promised to stay.

"Almost everyone has gone. There are only the old men left."

"If they are not too old to handle a cudgel they will do," I said, pointing to a grove of tall bamboo. "We will cut some of the green stalks. They make good weapons."

"Some of the women might come, too. They help my grandmother when there are many guests and are obliged to us."

"Women, boys, old men, it does not matter if there are enough of us."

"Go to the house over there." She pointed to a low hovel not far away. "There is a woman there I trust. She is a friend of Grandmother's. She will help."

I was glad of my new clothes and that I had washed. The clothes made me confident. There was another reason I wanted to stay: the man with the limp had said I should be careful because monkeys, too, can fall from a tree. I wanted to show him that I did not fall easily.

"Go back in there!" I ordered. "If he wants sake, do not

be stingy but give him full measure and more. If we can get him drunk, so much the better."

The woman looked a little like Aya-san. She had the same small bright eyes, like a bird. I told her about the visitor who had come to the inn and what I suspected his purpose was. Her house had only one room, but, as there was little to fill it, it appeared large. There was an earthen floor, and the old hen walking around inside seemed to consider itself one of the family. I got on with the woman immediately, so it had not been difficult to tell my story. She listened patiently, and when I finally finished, she said, "I think I know the man. If it is he, then you are probably right, for he was never any good to anyone. He got a sword cut in a fight, and that is how he became lame. Whoever wounded him left him for dead. I saw him here a few days ago. He used to live not far from here. He had a wife, but she drowned herself in the river. Some say he pushed her in, but that is hearsay and there is no reason to listen to that when there is enough else bad to tell about him."

"Would it be natural for you to have an errand at the inn?" I asked. "You could have a look at him without his suspecting anything."

"Oh, they are as used to seeing me as you are to seeing the sun in the sky." She laughed. "I have run in and out of the place since I was but a slip of a girl." She got up, pointed to some matting, and said, "You sit there and wait for me, boy." Grabbing a wide-brimmed straw hat which half hid her face, she left.

It did not take long before she was back. Beaming as if she brought good news she said, "Oh, that is him—the same no-good beggar. He is eating rice and drinking sake and looking as pleased with himself as the cock in the hen yard. I talked to Ume but not to her grandmother for I did not want him to see me. The old lady is very upset because her son has left with Lord Baba. She was praying to Buddha by her family shrine."

I wondered if Buddha or Oinari-sama or any of the gods ever cared what the people who prayed to them asked for. Somehow I felt certain that they did not listen at all. Perhaps they listened to the great lords, to Katsuyori or Lord Baba, but to those like myself, I felt certain that they did not. We had to survive on our own terms, not on theirs. "If we can get five or six people together to help, I think that will be enough," I said, looking at her inquisitively.

"That will not prove too difficult. The old lady is well liked." Suddenly she frowned; her good-natured face creased up as she tried to remember something. Not bothering to hold her hand in front of her mouth, she laughed and I noticed she had few teeth left, even though she was not so old. "I have been trying to recall his name ever since you came . . . it is Yosaku. Yes, Yosaku."

"He must not see me," I said, "for then he will guess that they have been warned. I met him on my way here."

"Don't worry! He looked so pleased with himself that I am sure he suspects nothing. My father will be coming soon. He likes nothing better than to waste time and money over there drinking sake. He and the old lady are as close as two plums on the same branch. He can tell her about your plan. The thought of a fight will please him. He finds the days too long and too dull."

She was right about her father. His eyes lit up as I told my tale. He was old and bent, so old that he had served Takeda Shingen's father, Nobutora. At first when he referred to the young master, I thought that he meant Katsuyori, but for him the young master was Takeda Shingen, the great warlord of Kai, who had died three years before aged over fifty. I never learned the old man's name. In my mind and sometimes in my speech I called him Ojiisan, Grandfather.

"I will get some of my friends. We will hide in the back kitchen and when they come we will smash them like flies on a hot summer day . . ." As Ojiisan said "Flies," he clapped his hands as if he had just caught one. I could not help laughing.

Most of his friends were younger, but all of them had spent at least sixty summers on earth. Ojiisan was like a general reviewing his troops. Some of them had come with weapons, rusty old knives and lances. Grandfather glanced at these in disgust. He agreed with me that bamboo cudgels would serve us best.

"What could one use that for?" He glanced at a knife an old fellow held forth. "It is not sharp enough to cut a rice cake. And that!" Ojiisan pointed to a lance an old man so bent with age that he saw more of the earth than the sky was holding. I was afraid he needed it to keep himself upright. "The shaft is so rotten that it would break if you hit a mosquito with it. We are going to cut bamboo cudgels for us all. I have decided that those are the best weapons. We don't want to kill them, merely to beat them so that they won't forget it in a hurry."

I could not help smiling but turned away to hide it. I did not mind hearing my own words in another's mouth. It was just as well to let the old man take over. After all, I was but a young child, a young monkey. I helped to cut the bamboo, and we made cudgels for all. They were about three feet long, and I would not care to be hit with one. Then the old man and one of his cronies went to the inn to drink sake and spy on the cripple. I was a little worried about that, wondering if I could trust the old man not to give everything away. I was afraid that once he had had a few cups himself, he might start talking and hinting about what should happen to thieves that come creeping in the night to disturb decent people in their slumber.

By the time the moon rose we were all packed into the back kitchen of the inn. It was hard to keep the old men from talking. One fell asleep, and we had to wake him because he snored. Ume had heated sake and made rice balls for them to munch. She had made up Yosaku's sleeping place as far as possible from the kitchen door. I wondered if he did not hear us because I knew he was not asleep but waiting for the others to come. The sake he had drunk would certainly have made him drowsy. It was a little after midnight when we heard an owl hoot or, rather, someone imitating the sound. It was a poor imitation, and one of the old men made a sound of disgust. He was admonished by an ever louder "Hush!" from our "general." I thought that surely Yosaku would hear us, but maybe he was a little deaf or drunker than we supposed, for the "owl" had to hoot several times before he got up. He tried to move as soundlessly as he could, but the sake had made him unsteady and near the door he almost fell.

The door squeaked loudly as he slid it back. He mumbled something as he stepped outside. Had he gone to warn the others that they had been betrayed? Maybe even to tell them that it was the little monkey who had spoiled their plans? If he had, then they would hunt for me until they found me. All of a sudden we could hear the low murmur of voices. They were at the entrance. They closed the outer door behind them. Someone said something, and the others laughed as they entered. They suspected nothing. They were not afraid.

9 *The Battle*

We did not stir, but let them enter. I heard the last of them close the door. They were all whispering. There was a full moon, so a very dim light came through the paper window-panes. Suddenly their leader—I recognized his voice—called out for a light. At that moment we all burst out from the kitchen like so many demons. One of the old men screamed, "Hurrah!" and the thump of the bamboo cudgels hitting the young robbers, who screamed as loud as they could, filled the room. "Murder! Murder!" I heard someone yell, as I walloped him as hard as I could. I wondered if the boy who had defended me when I was in their lair was among them. If he was I hoped he would escape, for I wished him no harm. A loud crash told me that some of the boys had broken down the sliding door and had escaped. Soon the moonlight illuminated the hole where the door had been, and the others followed. We were left victorious and with two prisoners. One was the cripple Yosaku; the other, one of the boys of the gang.

The cripple was lying very still. One of the old men kicked him, but he didn't move. "Bring some light!" the old man shouted. Ume brought a flickering oil lamp from the kitchen. A knife was still in Yosaku's chest, and blood was oozing out around the hilt.

"Whose knife is it?" Grandfather asked, looking at his "soldiers." They all shook their heads. "Is it yours?" Grandfather asked me.

"I have no knife." I looked more closely. The hilt was embossed with silver. It was a valuable weapon. "Is he dead?" I asked.

Grandfather knelt beside the wounded thief and drew the knife from the wound. No spurt of blood followed. The thief was dead.

Death is solemn. I had no use for the thief, and I am sure he would have killed, or seen any of us killed, without it bothering him, yet at that moment I felt sorry for him. That was the way my father had been killed. One moment filled with life and the next . . . Soldiers in the battlefield die in such a manner, life disappearing as the blood flows from them, changing them from men into corpses.

"I know whose knife that was," our prisoner declared. Two of the old men were holding him. It was the boy who had defended me.

"He is called Nezumi. They did not like each other. I heard him scream 'Traitor!' But I did not know he had killed him."

"He wasn't, you know. A traitor, I mean. But he was very foolish and drank too much sake and was not on his guard." I looked down at the dead man. "Is it true that his name was Yosaku and that he came from near here?"

"Yes, he was the one who told us that the old lady had

money, that she was rich." The boy did not act as if he knew me or had ever met me before. The oil lamp had been placed near the dead man's head, and in the faint light his profile looked handsome and his face wise. What would happen to him in his next life? Would he become a cockroach or maybe a rat?

"Get some rope and tie him up." Grandfather nodded toward the boy. One of the old men ran to fulfill his command.

"Ojiisan, what do we do with him?" I asked, pointing to the body of the man who had once answered to the name of Yosaku.

Ojiisan looked at the dead man, who was staring up into the ceiling as if he could see through it to the sky beyond. "Take him down to where the two roads cross and leave him there!" he ordered. Four of the old men carried the lifeless body out, holding it by its feet and hands. As they passed through the door I thought of the cripple's warning. It was he, not I, who had fallen from the tree.

The old fellow who had been sent for a rope returned and was busy tying up the young thief.

"He saved me once," I said and nodded toward him.

"What is your name?" demanded Ojiisan.

"Shiro." Humbly the boy bent his head. "My father was a soldier and is dead. My mother lives with her brother and works for him. I am her youngest son."

"Then why don't you live with her instead of with such scum?" Ojiisan looked angrily at the youngster. "How old are you?"

"This will be my thirteenth summer if I live that long." Again the boy bent his head. "My uncle has children of his own. He took my mother in out of charity but said there was no room for me as his house is very small."

Ojiisan grunted. He had no use for an uncle who would leave young kinsmen to starve. I could not help admiring Shiro. He was very clever. "If we let you go, will you promise to leave those . . ." Ojiisan stopped because he did not know what to call the young thieves he had so thoroughly beaten. "Thieving dogs," he finally said.

Shiro bent his head as slowly as he could. "I only stayed with them because I was hungry. I shall go to my uncle and beg him to take me in," he said and sighed. "And even if he will not, I shan't go back," he added. I could not help wondering if that uncle of his existed at all.

"If he will not take you in, then shame on him." Ojiisan obviously believed in the uncle. I could see his anger transferring from the young thief to his uncle, who was now, in his mind, the reason Shiro had become a thief. "He will end up giving him a few copper mons before he has finished," I thought and tried not to smile.

The men who had carried the dead thief away returned. They all sat down in a line in front of Shiro. Counting Ojiisan, there were seven in all. Sitting in the middle, Grandfather glanced first to the right and then to the left as he spoke. "Considering the age of this boy and that his father was a soldier, I think we should let him go."

The three on the right nodded their heads in agreement. But those on the left were not so easily satisfied. The bent old man spoke first.

"How do we know that he is not the one who owned the knife? How do we know that he is not their leader?"

"Young Saru here says he is not." Grandfather pointed at me.

"And who would listen to a monkey?" the old man asked scornfully. "You cannot grow plums on a pine tree," he proclaimed. At the sound of these words of wisdom, his two companions on the left nodded their heads gravely.

"If Saru here had not come and warned us, then it would be the robbers who would be sitting here drinking sake." Ojiisan glared at his rebellious soldiers. They, in turn, looked down at their empty hands, for, in truth, they had not been offered any sake. At that moment Ume and Grandmother appeared with a tray full of grilled river fish. Bowls of rice and sake cups were passed around.

"Please eat this fish, which is but poor fare for such valorous men as you. Until the end of time my family will be indebted to you all. I humbly beg of you not to be angry at this poor display but to eat heartily and forgive me for not being able to give you anything better."

The old men were very much inclined to forgive her, and they all started to eat most heartily. Soon, as they drank more than they ate, they began laughing and telling and retelling their part in the great "battle" of the inn. I, too, was eating. The fish was very good indeed, and the rice was mixed with mountain herbs, which made it very tasty.

"Untie the boy and let him eat as well," suggested Ojiisan.

There was a moment's silence until the old fellow on the right of Grandfather said, "Yes, untie the boy."

"So he can run away and rob someone else," mumbled the bent old man. When he felt that he was losing the support of his companions, he grunted: "Let him go for all I care, what is he to me? I have nothing he can steal."

Shiro was released. As soon as he was free, he knelt down and bowed to each of the old men in turn. Some of them smiled, pleased at the show of homage, but the old man who was so poor that he had no fear of being robbed made a grimace to make the boy understand that he was not taken in by his behavior.

Ume gave Shiro a bowl of rice but did not give him any fish. Though I guessed that the boy was very hungry, he ate the rice slowly, which made a good impression on all.

More sake was drunk, and some of the old men's faces got as red as the sun when it sets. Finally, Ojiisan decided that the party was over. He bowed and thanked Grandmother for the food and the sake, and the other old men added their thanks as well. One, who was a carpenter, said he would come and repair the door the next day. The old lady bowed in turn and declared that she was ashamed of the food she had served and that even the sake could have been of better quality but it was the best she had. This ritual took such a long time that one of the old men sat down in exhaustion. He had to be helped up and supported by two others on his way home.

As soon as they had all left, Sumi-san turned to me, declared her thanks, and asked me to stay until morning. "You can sleep there," she said, pointing to the bed which had been made up for Yosaku. Then a little confused, she turned toward Shiro, not knowing what to say to him.

"Let him sleep here until morning as well," I said. "He saved me once when I was in trouble."

Sumi-san frowned, but as she looked out through the broken door into the dark night she relented and agreed.

Shiro and I lifted the damaged door up and leaned it against the walls to cover most of the hole. "It will keep foxes and Tanukis out," I said with a grin.

"And monkeys inside," replied Shiro and laughed. Once we were lying in the bedding that had kept Yosaku warm, I asked: "Do you have an uncle?"

Shiro chuckled, "Certainly, whenever I need one."

"I thought so," I answered and closed my eyes.

Shiro

Never had I slept so comfortably in my whole life. Straw had been spread and on top of that a thin mat. As a covering we had been given a man's winter kimono. I was warm and half asleep. I turned, expecting to find Shiro next to me, but I was alone. "He has gone off in the night, probably stealing what he could lay his hands on," I thought. But then I heard his voice and that of Ojiisan's as well. I stretched and opened my eyes just enough to realize that it was already long since the sun had risen. Someone was hammering. Then I recalled the old man who was a carpenter and who had promised to come and repair the door. I closed my eyes again. I wanted to enjoy the warmth for just a little while longer. I could not make out what Ojiisan was saying. He sounded almost as solemn as the priest in the temple. Suddenly I remembered poor Neko and decided that I would ask Ume to give me a little of the fish from yesterday if there was any left over. From the cat my thoughts jumped to the old Samurai. He had probably expected me back yesterday. Now he would be angry at me and probably not even pay me. Half asleep, I argued with him and pointed out the danger I had been in for his sake. He didn't seem to care but ordered his servant to throw me out. So vividly did I imagine all this that I was still furious as I sat up. Then I realized it had only been a dream.

"So he has finally woken up—but too late for breakfast." Shiro laughed.

"Oh no, Ume will give him something." Ojiisan looked upset at the thought that I should be cheated out of my breakfast. Sitting up, I ran my hands through my hair.

"Someone like Ojiisan is a poor man," I thought, "yet every day he has something to eat and at night he sleeps on a straw mat well covered and warm."

"Ume!" Ojiisan called. When the little girl came he said: "Saru is awake, he will want some breakfast."

Ume looked at me. I think she had heard Shiro say it was too late for breakfast, for she declared there was no more rice, as they had eaten it all. Ojiisan, who had had two bowls full of rice, was crestfallen. But Ume could not keep a straight face, and he realized they were joking. As he laughed, his eyes—which were never very large—became mere slits.

You could not help but like Ojiisan. Perhaps it was because he was so old that he had returned to the openness of a child. He would say things as he thought of them, without worrying if saying them would hurt his dignity. Age had not made him foolish. It had loosened, or even cut, the bonds that seem to bind most grownups.

I ate two bowlfuls of rice and had one egg. This was a gift from Ojiisan, which he pointed out with some pride. I recalled the hen I had seen walking around inside his house as I thanked him. I was given a little fish as well, which I put aside, planning to save it for Neko. But Ume noticed this and, guessing my reason, told me she had saved some fish heads and other scraps for my cat. Bowing my head in thanks, I thought I would like to stay in the inn forever.

"Are you going to see your uncle?" I asked as Shiro and I walked back toward Kofuchu.

"My uncle?" Shiro looked at me in surprise. Then, recalling the story he had told Ojiisan, he laughed. "There is no uncle, and if there were, I am not sure he would take in my mother."

"You can't go back. They will believe it was you who told!"

"No, I won't go back. I had thought of leaving anyway. Nezumi is a fool, and it is only a matter of time before someone will cut his head off to decorate a stake. I might go back to Ojiisan." Shiro grinned.

"Go back to Ojiisan," I repeated, not understanding what he meant.

"He told me that if my uncle kicked me out, I could come to him." Shiro picked up a stone and threw it. "Don't you like him?" he asked.

"Very much," I said and felt envy tearing inside my breast like an imprisoned bird. "Why had he not asked me?" I thought as I looked at Shiro. He was a good-looking boy, not small like me; his nose was prominent, not tiny and almost flat like my own.

"He has no grandchildren—his daughter never married. He could adopt me." Shiro glanced at me.

"What about your own father, the one who was killed?" I felt it was robbing that dead soldier if he allowed Ojiisan to adopt him. Shiro laughed, picked up another pebble, and sent it flying into the sky.

"He won't care any more than my uncle will."

"You mean you don't have a father?" I asked in surprise. Then, because I was still such a child, I added, "But everyone has a father."

"That is true, and presumably I have one as well. He may well have died in the battle of Mikata-ga-hara. So no one can accuse me of lying." Shiro's face, which had been as clear as the summer sky, was suddenly overcast, and he said angrily: "My mother has one of the little inns where more than sake is sold. She would not know which of her guests was my father."

I did not really understand but sensed at least that it was best to say nothing, and we walked in silence for a while.

By the stone Jizo where I had rested on my way to the inn we sat down. "Sometimes I dream that some important Samurai was my father—even Takeda Shingen himself." Shiro laughed a bitter laugh.

"I never knew mine, not really. When the Takeda army left I watched it and tried to imagine what my father must have looked like. He carried a lance and belonged to Naito's troops. I saw the lord himself, riding a black horse."

"Every time a soldier is killed, some woman is made a beggar and some children are left to starve." Suddenly Shiro laughed. "Do you know what Ojiisan said to me?"

I shook my head and looked at him expectantly.

"He told me that he wished he was young, for this was the time when even such as he could become great. He said that

Lord Toyotomi had been but a common soldier like himself."

"Lord Toyotomi." I repeated the name. "Who is he?" I asked, feeling terribly foolish and young because of my ignorance.

"You have never heard of Lord Toyotomi Hideyoshi?" Shiro asked incredulously.

"No." I shook my head, trying to remember if the priest at the temple had ever mentioned him. "I should have listened to him more attentively," I thought guiltily. The trouble was that my world was much too small to contain such great lords. It consisted of the fight to get enough to eat, keeping warm, and my cat, Neko. I was very wise for my age, but still a small child. My innocence made Shiro laugh.

"However did you survive? You should have died and been thrown into the river for the fish to eat." He shook his head in wonder. "Lord Toyotomi has risen to his rank from very low, better than you and me but still not much. He and Lord Oda and Lord Tokugawa are the mightiest rulers in the land since our lord Takeda Shingen died. At present they are friends. Men may share a bowl of rice but seldom power."

I was chewing on a blade of grass and found everything Shiro said wonderfully clever. Then I recalled a name and to show that I was not totally ignorant I asked, "Lord Uesugi, is he not a great and powerful lord?" Uesugi Kenshin was the ruler of Echigo, the next province. The priest at the temple admired him.

"He is only an overgrown Bushi, a Samurai who loves his two swords and thinks the whole world is mirrored in their shiny blades. He likes to fight, as a wrestler likes to wrestle or a hunter to hunt, but it has no purpose." Shiro laughed disdainfully.

"And who will win, of the three lords whose names I have already forgotten?" I asked.

"Oda Nobunaga would have your head chopped off for asking that. He is the most unwilling to share power. He is vain and arrogant. Lord Toyotomi Hideyoshi is cunning but not as shrewd as the third. If I should choose to serve one of them it would be Tokugawa Iyeyasu."

"Why don't you?" I suggested, thinking it an easy thing to go and serve a lord.

"First, I live in Kai and Tokugawa is an enemy of our lord. Second, the time is not right and I am too young."

"But you have finished with the rat, so what will you do in Kofuchu?" I thought of asking him to share my little temple but did not dare suggest it.

"I shall go and see my mother. She will not be pleased to see me, but if she has money she will give me some. Then I shall return to Ojiisan and stay with him until the time is ripe."

I did not ask him for what the time had to be ripe. I thought I knew.

"What will you do?" he asked, stopping for a moment to look at the stone figure. "Jizo-sama, take care of this child," he said and pointed to me so that the little god should understand whom he meant.

I bowed to him and to the Jizo, giving respect to both. "I shall go and see the old Bushi who sent me on the errand. But first I will go to the little shrine where I live and feed my cat. Ume gave me fish for him."

"I shall come and see you tomorrow before I leave. Did the old woman in the inn give you anything?"

"She gave me two mon." I held out the copper coins. "Would you like one of them?" I asked.

"No. I was going to ask you if you wanted one of mine. Ojiisan gave me three." The thought that at the same time we had both had the intention of sharing our money made us both laugh.

At the entrance to the city we parted. I stood still and watched him until he turned the corner and was lost to view.

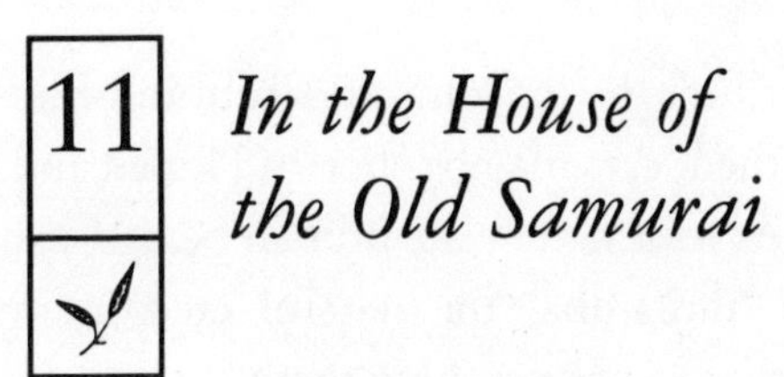

11 *In the House of the Old Samurai*

As I came near the little shrine to Oinari-sama, I began to fear that something had happened to Neko. I ran the last of the way and there he was, curled up in the sunshine near one of the little stone figures of a fox which flanked the shrine. "Neko!" I cried. The cat opened his eyes and stretched himself before jumping toward me. I picked him up and stroked him. "Neko, I have fish for you," I said, and the cat gave a loud miaow. He had already smelled it.

"I am very stupid and ignorant," I said as I watched Neko gulp down the food. "I don't know anything at all, Neko." The cat turned his head to look at me and then continued eating. "You are only a cat so all you have to know is how to catch mice or rats. Maybe I will ask the priest in the temple to teach me to read." The thought excited me for a moment. I knew a few of the Chinese characters, but there were thousands of them to learn. The priest had once shown me the signs for Amida Buddha and told me that the signs had come from China in the very, very old times, hundreds and hundreds of years ago. "I think it is better to be a cat," I said and petted Neko, who had finished eating and was now showing his gratitude by purring and rubbing himself up against me. But then, cats may be shot and killed and even, I was told, eaten. At least no one ate human beings, except the mountain witch Yamamba, the hateful creature who led travelers astray, then caught and ate them.

I kept putting off going to see the old Samurai because I was frightened of him. Samurais held such power over us all that my fear was neither foolish nor unreasonable. Our lives meant so little to them that they could end them for no reason at all. We knew them, we had to, they were the dangerous animals in our woods. But they did not know us, did not notice us, except to curse us if we got in their way or to demand that we serve them.

I thought of not going at all since the message I was bringing was not the one he wanted. Finally, late in the afternoon, I set out. His house was not so grand nor were there many servants about. One finally deigned to notice me and asked roughly what I wanted. Servants always seem to take on all the worst qualities of their masters; if the master is arrogant, then you can be sure the servants are twice as haughty.

"I have been on an errand for your master," I said. "He asked me to come back."

"A likely story, and what kind of errand was that?" The fellow was surly and rude. "If I disturb my master for nothing, I will catch it," he said, making no attempt to move.

"He asked me to come back. I have a message for him," I repeated and stood my ground.

"Stay here and don't go nosing around and putting things

which do not belong to you in your sleeve." He called a boy a few years older than me. "Watch this child of a river rat, and see that he steals nothing."

I do not know what I could possibly have stolen since I was standing outside the entrance to the house. The boy who was to guard me grinned insolently. Standing with his arms akimbo, he demanded to know my name and where I came from.

"From down by the river. They call me Saru," I said.

"Monkey!" The boy laughed. Then, for no reason at all, he poked my shoulder with his fist. Not so hard that it really hurt but hard enough for me not to mistake it for friendliness. I stepped back to be out of reach of his fists.

"Didn't you hear? He told you to stay where you are and not go nosing about. Come back!"

"Not if you are going to hit me," I said.

"Come back!" he commanded and pointed to a spot on the ground in front of him.

"What are you doing?" the servant demanded. The boy's face grew red.

"I am teaching him not to be cheeky," he said and gave me an angry look.

"You need lessons in that yourself," the servant mocked. "Follow me!" he said, motioning with his hand toward the door.

In the dim light of the room the old Samurai looked even more ancient. His skin was stretched like paper on the bones of his face.

I knelt in front of him and bowed very low. The old man said nothing but looked at me with anticipation.

"My Lord, the young man has gone to fight. He is with Lord Baba's troops. His mother was alone in the inn."

"I expected you yesterday." The old Samurai looked at me as if I were a fly and he was deciding whether to swat me or not.

"I am sorry." I looked as downcast as I could, which was not so difficult since I thought that I had lost any hope of a reward.

"What kept you?" Slowly, the old Samurai smiled. "Were there so many nuts in the tree that the monkey did not feel like climbing down?"

"No, My Lord, there was a fight at the inn. We were attacked."

The old Bushi's smile widened into a grin. "And who did you fight? And did you get beaten?"

I decided it was best to tell the whole story, leaving out only the part of where the robbers' house was. For, though I did not like them, I had no real wish to see them harmed. As I told my story I was surprised to see the old man's eyes light up just as Ojiisan's had. "They are terribly bored, these old men," I thought. "No one pays any attention to them anymore. Everything they prize and are proud of belongs to a past which is quickly forgotten by those around them." When I had finished my story, I bowed once more.

"You are a clever monkey, Saru. The name fits you. I should like to have seen that battle—all the old men banging away with their bamboo cudgels, probably recalling when they had had better weapons than that. How old are you?"

"I shall be eight this summer."

"Eight years. That is a long time at your age. Now the years fly by like snowflakes in winter, and with little more substance to them either. Here." The old Samurai took a little purse from his sleeve and drew out a silver ryo.

"Thank you, My Lord." I bowed so low that my forehead touched the floor.

"Goro!" he called, and the servant who had led me in appeared so quickly that I was sure he had been listening beyond the door.

"Yes, Master." He bowed and stood waiting instructions.

"If Saru should come again, do not turn him away before I have seen him." Then he said to me, "Let me know, Saru, if you are ever in danger of falling out of your tree." He smiled and indicated that I could leave.

I thanked him in a whisper and bowed for the last time. The old Samurai had already turned away. "I wonder where he is now," I thought, for the old are always dreaming of something which happened long ago. They live in the past as the young men live in the future. Only children like myself live in the present.

The servant led me out but did not speak to me again. At the door he pointed to the gate of the compound, letting me know I was to leave. At the gate I turned to look back. The servant had already gone inside, and the place looked deserted. I was doubly surprised when a voice loudly commanded me to kneel as I stepped outside the gate.

It was the boy who had tried to torment me before. I did not kneel but looked down the street, wondering if I could outrun him.

"Kneel!" he repeated and pointed to the ground.

I shook my head, ready to duck if he tried to hit me. I knew that if I knelt all would be lost.

"Did he give you something?" the boy demanded. "Then give it to me!" He held out a hand.

"He gave me nothing." I lied. I was not going to give up my silver coin. I had never owned something as valuable as that.

"You are lying." Suddenly the boy's hand shot out and slapped my face. It was so unexpected that I did not manage to duck. The slap stung me, and I could feel my cheek growing red.

"I shall tell your master that you have been hitting me and trying to rob me!" I proclaimed in a voice which was not altogether steady.

"My father would never allow you in again. Give me whatever Akiyama gave you, and I will let you go."

I pretended to look for something in my clothes. Just then, as he turned away to see if anyone was watching us, I darted away. Never before had I run so fast. Not far away the street joined a larger one. Once there I would be safe.

I do not know when the boy gave up his pursuit, for I just kept running, darting in and out among the crowd on the main street, and did not stop until I had reached the temple where I knew the priest.

At the shabby gate to the little temple I finally halted. I was out of breath and sat down on the steps. "I will pray to Oinari-sama that he will break his neck," I said to myself. "And his father, too," I added and laughed.

I said that I hated the Samurais, but that is not whom I

hated most. I hated their servants even more; more arrogant than their masters, they blew themselves up with pride until they were many times their natural size. They were like the kites you see flying on a windy day: big as eagles in the sky but held by a string and made out of a few sticks and some colored paper. I felt the silver coin I had tucked into the secret little pocket of my new jacket. It was still there, together with the two mon the innkeeper had given me. At that moment I realized that Shiro—who had been part of the gang of robbers—had gotten one more mon from Ojiisan than I, who had saved them from the robbers. The thought made me grin. I did not mind. Especially not now, when I had a whole ryo to show and brag about to Shiro.

12 *The Wounded Soldier*

It was midsummer when the news of Katsuyori's defeat at Nagashino finally reached Kofuchu. Almost every household in the town had either a father or son in the Takeda army. Was he among the survivors, or did he lie dead in some field far, far away? The women looked at each other wondering if they were widows, the children if they were fatherless. There would be many beggars that year who could shout to indifferent passersby, "My father was killed at Nagashino."

Being a proper orphan and knowing no one in the army, I was not so concerned about Katsuyori's defeat. He was a great lord and I a human fly; his concerns were not mine nor mine his.

I expected Shiro to come to my "house" as I had told him about the little shrine to Oinari-sama. But many days passed and became weeks, and no Shiro appeared. He was the first friend that I had ever had, and I felt terribly hurt. Finally, I decided to go back to the inn and ask if they had seen him. I bought a fried fish in one of the stalls, ate half of it, and gave the other half to Neko. I explained carefully to him that I was going away for the day and he would have to take care of himself. If I had not had the cat I think I should probably have talked to myself, like the lonely old people you sometimes see, muttering as they stagger along. I felt that Neko understood what I said. Sometimes he answered, giving a loud miaow, when I finished speaking.

It was a lovely day. On the way to the inn I washed in the river. There was not much water, but I found a pool deep enough so that the water covered me. Lying there I thought of the girl in the tavern. She was partly the reason for my sudden desire for cleanliness. I recalled that she had ordered me to wash and that I had been embarrassed. I said her name aloud and splashed the water with my feet. The sun caught the spray and made a rainbow in it. I wondered if her uncle had died at Nagashino among Lord Baba's troops. I thought about the leader of the gang of boys who had killed the cripple. In my mind's eye I saw him clearly, as he had looked when he had pressed the point of his knife against my throat. Could he have killed Shiro? I wondered and opened my eyes. Further down the pool in the riverbed a hungry little white heron was fishing. The bird stood immobile in the water. All of a sudden its head darted down and came up with a small fish in its beak. Would Nezumi have the patience of the little heron to wait until he could kill Shiro? "No," I thought. He was a rat, and rats are restless animals. But surely he would want to avenge himself, not only on Shiro but on me, too. I got up and sat on the shingle of the riverbed, letting the sun dry me. The stones had been worn round by the water. I picked up one to see how far I could throw it. With a splash it landed in the water not too far from the heron. The bird turned its head to see who the intruder was, then spread its wings and flew away.

When I got near the place with the three stone Jizos, where I had met the crippled thief, I was surprised to see a man resting against one of the statues, almost in the same position as the thief. But he is dead . . . could it be his ghost? It was almost noon, and the sun was shining brightly. Ghosts don't show themselves in the daytime but come out at night when the world grows dark. I stood still for a moment, staring at him. It was a young man, a soldier. He had been wounded, and his leg was bandaged. He was not a Samurai, but a mere foot soldier. He met my glance and smiled in so friendly a manner that I walked up to him.

"Sit down, young man, and rest yourself. Soon it will be cooler, and an evening breeze might even rise and refresh us. Have you far to go?"

"Not so far," I answered, sitting down opposite him. "Does your leg hurt?"

"It is only a scratch and will hardly leave a scar to brag about. The one who gave it to me aimed for my heart, I am sure, but either his eyes or his arrow was crooked since it hit my leg. I owe him my life for it and would gladly bow my head to the ground in giving thanks." The soldier patted his leg tenderly as he spoke.

"Would it not have been better if you had not been hit at all?" I asked in surprise.

"I was on guard the day before Katsuyori ordered the big attack. One of Tokugawa's or Nobunaga's men on watch got bored with sitting still and took up his bow. Seeing me, he decided I would make a handy target and shot off an arrow and hit me in the leg. The next day the battle took place when half the Takeda army was slaughtered. That battle will still be talked about when your grandchild is an old man. Since I was wounded the day before I was excused that mass seppuku . . . so here I am, still alive when I ought to be dead."

"My father was killed at Mikata-ga-hara," I said, adding foolishly: "he was killed by a spear in his chest, which means he didn't run away."

"A brave man. I admire brave men, maybe because I am not one myself. To die on the battlefield may be great, but what if you are reborn as a cockroach or a rat? I ran away as soon as the fighting was over, and I have been running since. That is why I am resting now."

"If everyone ran away like that, why there would be no battles," I said childishly.

"And what a great pity that would be! No widows to mourn you, no little orphans to beg—why, it would be a calamity! But the Samurais would fight, wouldn't they?"

"Yes, I suppose so." Then I realized the soldier was jesting. "But there would soon be no Samurais left," I said.

"And who would we kneel to then?" With mock seriousness the soldier shook his head. "That wouldn't do; there would be no one to kick us either."

"Oh, but there would be." I became serious. "There would be somebody who would call himself our master. There would always be someone to kick us."

The soldier smiled kindly at me. "You are too young to have thoughts like that. You should be playing with a bamboo sword and shooting arrows you have cut yourself. When night comes and your mother has bid you good night, you should be dreaming yourself a great warrior. You should . . ."

"I have no mother!" I shouted, interrupting him.

"Did she die at Mikata-ga-hara as well?"

"How could she—she was a woman," I said in annoyance.

"No, that is true—she couldn't have died in battle, could she? I tell you, on the battlefield, once they look at their own blood oozing out, the river of their life running dry, there is many a man who would change with his wife if he could."

"My mother died when I was born. I was told they cut me out of her belly."

"Yes, they too have their battlefield." The soldier sighed. "We all do, and if we don't, then we make one for ourselves."

I didn't understand what he meant, but I liked him. He was one of the first grownups who had really talked to me. The soldier looked up at the sky and then at me. "How old are you?" he asked.

"Eight years, I think."

"Eight years," he repeated slowly, contemplating the number. Then he asked my name.

"I don't really have any," I said and then, "Oh, I am sure I do. I just don't know it."

"I see." The soldier nodded as if what I had said made sense.

"I am sure my father must have given me a name, but he died before he could tell me what it was. Aya-san's husband called me Saru."

"Monkey." The soldier looked me over to see if the name fit. Then he asked, "Who is Aya-san?"

"She is dead, too. She died in the fire when I was six. Matsu died, too."

"You seem to be a dangerous person—everyone you know dies. Who was Matsu?"

"She was only a girl who belonged to Aya-san. My father paid Aya-san to take care of me, but when he died Aya-san kept me anyway."

"A kind woman, Aya-san."

"She used to beat us sometimes, but she was kind. She and Matsu ran one way and I another in the big fire. I ran for the river."

"That was clever of you." The soldier smiled.

"Where are you going?" I asked. If the soldier had asked me to, I would have followed him, for I was like a stray puppy ready to wag my tail at the sound of a kind word. But the soldier shook his head and muttered, "Far away," as if far away was a place you could reach like the name of a town.

"It has been a great pleasure talking to you, Saru-san, and I wish you luck." The soldier got up and stretched himself. "We have met like two little clouds in the sky. Maybe someday the winds will blow us together again." He bowed, then put his hand on my shoulder and pressed it gently. "Remember, always be happy that you are alive—it may be the only gift the gods will give you." He grinned and then struck out on the road to Kofuchu.

"What is your name?" I shouted after him.

He stopped and turned. "The one who lived!" he shouted back and set off again.

I did not get up right away but followed him with my eyes until I lost sight of him beyond a clump of trees. I wished he had taken me along. "The one who lived," I mused. Yes, to be that was probably the most important in a battle. With a sigh I got up and continued my journey.

13 *I Am Unwanted*

The first person I saw at the inn was Ume. "Oh, it is you," she said as she saw me. "My uncle is dead, and my grandmother is sitting dried-eyed, crying. What do you want?"

"I want to know if you have seen Shiro. He promised to come to my place, but he didn't."

"He was here a couple of days ago. Maybe he is staying in the old man's house. I don't know, and I don't care either."

I was still too young to understand that when somebody says, "I don't care," it usually means they do care. "How do you know that your uncle is dead?"

"A lot of stragglers are coming back from the battle. One stopped here to tell us. I think he thought he ought to be rewarded for bringing such news, but I gave him nothing. Grandmother has been moaning and crying ever since. She ran out of tears last night, but that hasn't stopped her." Ume looked with disgust in the direction of the house, where her grandmother was mourning.

"Maybe he was lying," I suggested. "Maybe he didn't know for sure."

"Oh, he knew all right. He brought back an amulet that

Grandmother bought last fall at the temple. She recognized it. She hung it around my uncle's neck herself."

"They are all alike, everyone wears one."

"It was by the string that Grandmother knew it. It was a purple one from the obi of her marriage kimono."

I bowed my head in understanding, then asked, "What will happen now?"

"I don't know." Ume looked sullenly at me as if I were partly responsible for their difficulties. "If Lord Baba lets us stay, all will be well. I can take care of everything." She gave me a look, perhaps thinking I was going to dispute her ability to run the inn.

"Who will ferry people across when the river is up?" I asked, because for that work one needed strength.

Ume looked away, and I was sorry I had asked. "I can get plenty of men for that," she said contemptuously. "Maybe you would like to do it?" She grinned.

"I am not strong enough," I answered meekly. "I think Lord Baba was at Nagashino; maybe he was killed there. I have just talked to someone who came back from there. He said that more than half the soldiers in the Takeda army are dead."

"That would just mean we belong to someone else. Lord Baba stopped here once and Grandmother served him sake." Ume laughed. "She was so nervous at the honor that she spilled half of it. When he left she didn't bow but stretched herself right out upon the ground and scared his horse so he almost fell off."

"Your grandmother told me I was going to live to be an old man," I said, recalling my first meeting with her.

"She is crazy." Ume looked down at the toes of her bare feet. "Ever since her husband died she has been crazy. My grandfather was nice, I liked him. He was always laughing. When I was small he used to throw me up into the air and then catch me. He died coming back from Kofuchu. Someone robbed him and killed him. Since then the old lady has not been right in the head, and now that my uncle is dead as well, that is the last of her sons. All she has left now is me . . . and I am only a girl."

"There will be many like her," I said, as if that were a consolation. "I don't think Lord Baba will bother about the inn though. If he is still alive, he will have other things to think about."

"I think so, too." Ume smiled. "If only Grandmother would stop! Crying won't bring my uncle back." She spoke in a matter-of-fact tone and glanced toward the inn for a moment.

"Oh, she will stop. No one has cried forever. What was your uncle like?"

"I didn't like him." Ume scowled. "He was always drinking sake and using all Grandmother's money. She spoiled him; she would have torn out her heart for him. Why do women always like boys better than girls?"

"I don't know if they do. My mother died when I was born."

"My own mother was ashamed because she did not have a son. She often said to me, 'You should have been a boy.' How could I help what I was? It is not my fault that I am not a boy. Grandmother said the other evening, looking at me, 'If only I had a grandson.' I think daughters are better. At least they don't become soldiers and get killed."

"What was your father like?" I asked, hoping that he, at least, had cared for Ume.

"I was so young when he died that I don't remember him. But I am sure he wanted me to be a boy, too, since he was a man. But why do women want boys? That's what I ask."

"Maybe because the men want them. They want boys, too, to please their husbands," I suggested. I felt far from certain that this was true and was only too willing to retract it if Ume disagreed.

"They will do anything to please their men." Ume knitted her brow. "Grandmother would, too."

"Ume!" A faint voice called from inside the inn. Then, when no one responded, the voice called again, this time a little louder. When the old lady called for the third time, Ume got up. "She is better now. Maybe she has stopped crying," she said. "I will see what she wants."

I stayed where I was, watching a bird circling over the river. Then, perhaps because I had been looking at a bird, I thought of the pheasant. The male pheasant has such colorful plumage, and the female is so very plain and dull. At least we are not like that, I thought, born so different. My thoughts drifted to other problems. I wondered why Shiro had not come to my place and why Ume sounded as if she were angry with him. Suddenly the bird dived down into the river and came up with a fish in its claws. It has caught its dinner, I thought, wondering if Ume would offer me some food or if I would be treated like the soldier who had informed them of her uncle's death. It was because she did not like her uncle that she would not give the soldier anything to eat, I decided. She was a strange girl. In some ways she behaved more like a boy, but perhaps that was because her mother had wanted a boy instead of a girl. I had heard that in some cases if a family had too many girls they would set the newborn baby out in the mountains for Yamamba to eat. On the whole I was glad that I was born a boy and not a girl. If even as a boy I was not wanted, then if I had been a girl it would have been doubly so.

"She is hungry." Ume stuck her head out of the door of the inn. "Come! You can have something as well." I was barefoot, so I had no footwear to take off. The shutters had not been opened, and the room was in half darkness. The old lady was sitting by the family shrine, talking so softly to herself that I could not understand what she said. I could hear Ume in the lean-to kitchen, so I ran there soundlessly, for I was afraid of the old lady and did not want her to hear me.

I had just finished eating a portion of millet porridge when Shiro arrived. He did not seem the least bit surprised to see me. Taking a quick look at me, he seated himself across from me, as if the inn were his home. Ume dished him out some porridge and asked me if I wanted more. There was a little rice mixed in the porridge and some beans, and I was still hungry. To my surprise, I heard myself say "No" and even declare that I had had enough.

"Why did you not come to see me?" I asked Shiro, wishing I had stayed in Kofuchu and not come at all.

"I thought I better not." Shiro stopped eating long enough to glance at me, then continued eating.

"I waited for you," I declared miserably.

Shiro nodded, as he ate the last few mouthfuls and put down his bowl. "They were after me. I thought they might be following me, and I would lead them to your little shrine. He has declared that he is going to kill us both. Maybe you had better stay here."

"Who is he?" Ume asked.

"Nezumi, the leader of the gang. He has sworn that either he or I am going to die. I think it is going to be he."

"You should have let me know."

"Maybe." Shiro looked at me. "But what if I had led them right to your place? Nezumi would have cut your head off, and you wouldn't be here eating Ume's food."

"No, and neither would you." I felt hurt and disappointed. He had been my first friend, or so I had thought. "Are you staying with Ojiisan?" I asked.

Shiro nodded. "You can stay there, too, or maybe Ume will let you stay here."

"I would have to ask Grandmother." Ume sounded as if she had no wish to ask the old lady or for me to stay.

"You need not bother," I said, glancing at Ume and letting my gaze rest on Shiro. "I shall be going back to my own place. My cat is there."

"Let the cat catch its own mice." Shiro grinned as if he had said something witty.

"No," I said, getting up. "I couldn't leave Neko. He has kept me warm all winter." "A stray kitten—that is what I am to him," I thought. He didn't care what became of me. I walked through the main room of the inn as soundlessly as I could, but not silently enough, for the old lady heard me and called me. Momentarily I thought of acting as if I had not heard her and making my escape.

Silently I knelt in front of the old woman and waited for her to speak. Searchingly she studied my face, then she smiled a bitter smile.

"I remember you. You were the boy who came the night the robbers attacked. I gave you some of my son's clothes."

"Yes, and I am very grateful for them and sorry to hear of your bad news."

"That was the last of my sons, and my husband is dead, too. Everyone is dead, all of them killed." The old lady sighed. I noticed that her porridge bowl was standing empty on the floor. "She has been eating," I thought and said: "Ume is still here. She is a good girl."

"Ume only cares about Ume." The old lady grunted. "Are you going to stay here just like the other boy?"

I shook my head, then, because in the darkened room she might not have seen this, I said, "No, I shall be going back to Kofuchu."

"He is going to die, too." The old lady found this satisfying enough to bear repeating. "Yes, he is going to die as well."

"Who?" I could not help asking.

"The Takeda boy," she said with contempt.

"Katsuyori!" I exclaimed. Although I did not like what I heard or knew about him, I had never thought of our lord, our ruler, as "the Takeda boy."

"He will die a miserable death when all have left him." The old woman showed her toothless gums in a joyless smile.

"I must go now," I said and rose. The old lady seemed not to notice. Maybe she had forgotten me, I thought, as I bowed. I was almost at the door when a voice commanded. "Wait. Come here!"

I returned and again knelt in front of the old lady. "I like you better than the other boy," she declared. And then drawing a purse from inside her kimono, she opened it and peered in. "Take these!" she said and dropped three copper mons into my hand.

"Thank you very much," I said and bowed my head so low that my forehead touched the floor. "Thank you very much."

When I was outside again in the sunlight, I tucked the money away and then ran so far that I no longer could see the inn. I sat down on the riverbank. "It was from spite that she gave me the money," I said aloud. "She knew that Shiro and Ume were listening." I picked up a little stone and threw it as far as I could. I almost felt like crying. I couldn't leave Neko, I thought, and they didn't want me. It hurt and maybe because it hurt, I repeated it aloud: "They didn't want me."

I sat long by the riverbank, so long that the shadows had grown large by the time I rose. "I am not afraid," I thought, "even of dying," as I made my way back to the road. When I passed the three Jizos I half expected to find someone sitting there, but no one was. I bowed to the three stone gods and asked them to take care of me. When I came to the little Oinari-sama shrine, it had grown dark. Neko heard me coming and ran to meet me.

14 *I Get a New Home*

The day after my unsuccessful visit to the inn, the priest at the temple hailed me and told me that a friend of mine had come to ask for me the day before.

"I have no friends," I growled sourly and then asked what my "friend" had looked like.

"I did not like him, Saru," he declared. "I do not think you should have anything to do with him." He went on to give a very clear description of Nezumi.

"He said he was a friend of mine?"

"He did, Saru, but I sent him packing and did not tell him where you live. Is he your friend?"

"He is not. If he caught me he would kill me." I sat down on one of the wooden steps leading up to the temple. "His name is Nezumi, and he is a rat—a rat that bites." I told the priest about how I had met Nezumi and how I had helped defend the inn when he and his gang had attacked it.

"You should go away for a while," the priest suggested when he heard my tale.

"To where?" I asked. Recalling what had happened the day before, I said in a miserable tone of voice, "No one wants me."

"Why should anyone want you?" The priest sat down on the steps beside me. I looked at him in surprise. He smiled and repeated his question: "Why should anyone want you?"

"I don't know," I said. I could feel the tears pressing, but I held them back. "I don't know why anyone should. All I know is that no one does . . ."

"What about your cat?" the priest asked.

"A cat doesn't count," I said with disgust. I really was very fond of Neko, so I added, "The cat has no one but me to take care of him."

"Do you know how, or rather why, I came to serve Buddha?" the priest asked. When I shook my head he answered the question. "Because I was hungry."

"You were poor," I stated, looking at the priest.

"We were a large family. I had four brothers. What happened to them I do not know. There were two sisters as well, but they died. There were many, too many, mouths to fill and not enough to fill them. You know if there are too many birds in a nest, the stronger birds push out the weaker ones. I was one of the weaker ones."

"But now you have enough to eat." I smiled. "Even enough to give away."

"It is now years since I have gone to bed hungry, but I can still remember what it felt like. When you are a novice they don't feed you well either, but to me those simple meals were like a feast." The priest grinned as he recalled it. "I had fourteen years of hunger within me that had to be satisfied. Later I decided that if I prayed to Buddha long enough, he would reward me in my next life by making me a mighty lord, a great ruler of a province like ours. So from vanity I prayed, and Lord Buddha laughed in his heaven. Then one day I thought, as I watched a cockroach scurrying across the floor of the kitchen in the temple where I served, that maybe the cockroach in its former life had been just such a lord. When he had the power he had misused it, and wouldn't I do the same if I had been born to wealth and power? I had to answer yes, for all my dreams had been but vain and foolish, trapping myself in the mantle of a lord, like some foolish boy dressing himself in his father's armor."

"I have never thought about anything like that." I shook my head and laughed. "What was my cat, Neko, in his last life?"

"A foolish woman who spent too much time staring at her own reflection in a mirror." The priest smiled. "Cats are like that, always preening themselves."

"That is true, poor little Neko is always washing himself. But if he had a mirror to look into he must have been rich."

"If the cockroach I saw had been a great lord, then your cat could have been his wife," the priest suggested.

"I am not sure that your evil lord becomes a cockroach in his next life, or his wife becomes a cat. I think they become someone like Nezumi, and the evil stays inside them. I don't believe you are rewarded or punished in your next life." I bent down and picked up a little stone from the ground. "Your soul is like this stone. When you die it flees from you." I threw the stone in the air. It fell not far from the steps. "Where it falls is chance. You may become a great lord's child or someone like me, born to be of no importance."

"Saru, you are a clever little monkey. I agree with you. I

have had the same thoughts myself. The idea that you can become a cockroach or a rat in your next life is only a tale made up to frighten you into behaving. It has not worked, for surely if it had there would be less evil about."

"I have always been too busy just getting enough to eat and in the winter keeping warm to have such thoughts." I picked up another pebble, threw it into the air, and caught it as it fell.

"You see, the whole point of becoming a Buddha is that it is reward enough. That is why it is worth striving for. The reward of goodness and wisdom is goodness and wisdom, not something else. You are not like courtiers at the emperor's palace in Kyoto, who are given silk costumes and funny hats as rewards for good behavior. The reward is that there is no reward or any necessity for one."

I did not really understand what he meant, but I nodded anyway because I sensed that what he said meant much to him. For a while we both sat silently. One of the hens he kept came and picked at the hard summer earth near our feet. I wondered what it could find to eat there, and then about Nezumi and whether he would manage to kill me. I had no weapon to defend myself with, but I still had the silver ryo. Maybe it would buy me a knife.

As if the priest had guessed what I was thinking, he suddenly said, "I think you had better come and stay here. Your little shrine would not be safe."

I had never told the priest where I lived and was surprised that he knew. Perhaps if he knew, my home may have been more common knowledge than I thought. "Where could I stay here?" I asked, looking around me.

"One of the sheds can be locked from the inside. At least you will not be taken by surprise. I live in the hut not far from the shed myself. If you holler loud enough I should hear it."

"He is not alone; he wouldn't come if he were. So it would be best for you to lock your door as well, and if I holler 'Help' to plug your ears so you will not hear me."

"He may not come at all. I told him you did not live here and that I did not know what ditch you slept in. I made certain that he thought I found you of little importance. As I told you, I did not like him. He looked me in the eyes all right, but that is not a good way to judge a person. Many a scoundrel has no trouble looking into an honest man's eyes. It was something else that I found distasteful. He smiled all the time, but his smile had neither gaiety nor humor in it. It was, I thought, the smile of cruelty that I was gazing at. Come and stay here. You can help me sweep and clean the temple. It is one of the poorest and smallest in Kofuchu, if not in all of Kai. Our statue to our Lord Buddha was not carved with great skill, but we have guardians at the gate that might protect us." The priest smiled.

I bowed my head gratefully and thanked him. I felt remorse because I had thought him a fool. To my shame, it was his very kindness which had made me think him so. I looked around the little compound of the temple. "This is a better home," I thought.

Advancement in life is always easier to take than reverses. My little hut was not only dry when it rained, but it had a wooden floor. True, it was rough and the planks uneven, but it was a lot better than the bare earth which I had slept on before. My bedding might not have suited a Samurai's son: it was two old straw raincoats and some sacking that had been used to pack rice. It was now summer and the nights were warm, but when winter came with rain and snow, I would be, if not warm, at least dry. Neko liked our new home as well. Sometimes he would chase the priest's hens and I would have to scold him. The priest had an old dog, which was toothless and lazy and did not mind my cat. I took care to sweep and keep not only the temple but the compound clean.

I was careful to watch out for Nezumi or for a member of his gang. Any child that came near the temple I looked upon as an enemy, for I could not recall what all the children in his gang had looked like. I did this not only for my own protection but for the sake of the priest as well. I felt responsible for him, even though I was only eight years old and he a grownup.

There was something childlike about the priest, and he could sometimes ask the strangest questions. Like when he asked me why anyone should want me. Children might ask questions like that, as there is still much they do not understand. But once you are no longer a child you quickly learn what others consider foolish questions and do not ask them.

"I wonder why soldiers obey, Saru?" He had just given a few coppers to a soldier who had returned crippled from the battle. "You know that Katsuyori-sama ordered them to attack again and again. Oda Nobunaga's soldiers had guns and fired from behind a fence that protected them. They were just sent out to be killed."

"Maybe they were too scared not to do it," I said. "What are guns like?"

"They shoot iron arrows that can go right through you, and they make a lot of noise. The people that have come in big ships from the end of the world brought them here."

"Why did Katsuyori-sama order them to attack once he saw what happened?" I asked.

"Oh, that is easily answered. He was too proud once he had lost not to lose everything. He was like a child who cannot get his kite to fly in the air and therefore breaks it. It was not a kite he broke, but men. Why did they obey?"

"Because it is always easier to obey than not to obey." I thought of the rat and his gang of boys. They would obey him even when they did not want to.

"You are right, Saru," the priest said. "It is always easiest to obey."

"I once met someone who did not obey." I thought of the wounded soldier I had talked to near the three Jizo statues and told the priest about him.

"I should like to have met him. In your life you will meet many people, Saru, but most will be like shadows that soon disappear. But a few will teach you something, say some words to you that, like seeds sown in the earth, will sprout in your mind and flower and bear fruit. Such men or women are rare. Treasure them when you meet them. The one who lived . . . that is a fine name." The priest walked away shaking his head in wonder at my story.

15 A Visit from a Friend of Nezumi

"Is this your cat?" The girl who spoke was holding Neko by the scruff of his neck. Unused to such treatment, the cat was mewing loudly, his little legs clawing the air.

I looked at her. She was at least twelve or thirteen years old and stronger than me. "Put him down," I said casually.

"Nezumi told me to kill him. Shall I kill him?" The girl laughed.

"How did you guess he was my cat?" I asked, wondering if she would let go of Neko if I hit her.

"I found out where you live, too—in the little shrine." Again the girl laughed as if it were some kind of joke.

"Why should he want you to kill Neko?" I looked down at the girl's feet; they were bare and as dirty as my own.

"To teach you something."

"What would I learn from that?" I shrugged my shoulders as if I didn't care if she killed the cat.

"Teach you respect, that is what it would do. Teach you to be afraid."

"Don't you think I know how to be afraid? I have been as afraid as the cat is now many times." I grinned. "Have you seen the heads in the execution place, where they kill robbers like you and Nezumi? Some of them belong to thieves no older than you. Now they stare forever without ever seeing anything . . ."

"Nezumi is too clever for them!" the girl protested, but she did not sound as if she believed it.

"Let go of the cat!" I demanded, feeling that I had gained the upper hand.

She shook her head and started to swing the cat back and forth. Poor Neko's eyes were filled with terror.

I turned away as if I did not care what she did. Suddenly I swung back and with all my strength chopped her wrist with the side of my hand. With a scream she let go of Neko. He ran in under the temple to hide.

"You hurt me!" she said in surprise, rubbing her wrist. "I shall tell Nezumi."

"Tell him to leave me alone," I muttered and prepared myself for a fight.

"He will kill you." The girl's eyes were shiny with tears. "I will tell him what you did, and he will kill you."

"You can't cook the fish before it is caught." I laughed because I knew now that she wouldn't fight. "Leave then, before they catch you all and your head ends up on a stake."

The girl spat on the ground, then turned and walked away. I went to find Neko. It took me a long time to make him come out from his hiding place.

"Poor thing!" The priest looked thoughtfully at a branch of a tree growing near the entrance to the temple. "Wisdom comes too late to a fool. It is easy to see the folly of your ways once they have dragged you to your execution. I wish I had seen her. I would have talked to her."

"It would not have helped." I had told the priest about the girl's visit.

"You must never say that, Saru. Who knows? My words might have reached her." The priest shook his head. "If one could not lead her to the way of Buddha, one could at least have led her away from the road she is traveling on. It is easy to become a thief if you are poor enough—those who have slept with full bellies all their lives seldom think of that."

I had been rather proud of my handling of the girl and still remembered her treatment of my cat. "They might come here and burn the temple," I said.

"There will be many more of her kind now." The priest sighed. "Evil times will come to our province. We dreamed that Kai would rule Japan, and now that our dream is over, we wake to find ourselves in a nightmare. The roads of Kai will not be safe from bandits, starving Ronins who will dishonor their swords to fill their stomachs."

"She said she was going to kill my cat." I was still thinking about the girl, not about the state of affairs in our province—that was a matter for the grownups, not for me.

"She didn't hurt him." The priest smiled. He had forgotten that he was speaking to a child.

"She would have."

"How do you know?" The priest touched my shoulder.

"I know!" I declared, looking up at him. I could not have explained why I knew, but I felt certain that I was right. "She would have killed him!"

"Maybe. But I still feel sorry for her, Saru."

I shrugged my shoulders and walked away.

The girl believed that I still slept under the little shrine to Oinari-sama, but if they did not find me there they would look for me at the temple. Next day I went to the shrine. I wanted to clean the place underneath where I had slept. In front of the shrine were two little stone statues of foxes. To my surprise, they had been turned over and the bell rope that you pull to call the god and tell him you are there had been cut. I raised the two foxes. The one carrying the letter in its mouth had the tip of one of its ears broken off. I searched for the bell rope and finally found it, hanging over the branches of a tree. I tied it to the bell and shook it hard to make the bell ring loudly. "Oinari-sama, please give whoever did this bad dreams and make your little foxes bite them." The god did not answer, but then gods never do. I petted the fox who had lost the tip of its ear and cleaned up underneath the shrine. Now they will be able to see that I don't live here anymore and they will leave the little shrine alone. When I had finished, I prayed to Oinari-sama again, asking him to protect me. Though I did not believe in him any more than I believed in the stone Jizos, I felt it was safer to say the prayer. After all, I had been a guest of Oinari-sama all that winter and it might have been he who had kept me from harm.

I was about to return to the temple when suddenly I decided to spy on the house of Nezumi and his gang. I had no real reason for doing this. The town had been almost empty while Katsuyori was leading the Takeda army against his enemies. Now, after the defeat, it was once again filled with soldiers. The mood had changed. No longer was there any talk of victory, of Katsuyori becoming ruler of Japan. All illusions were gone. The men who had celebrated future victories now celebrated future defeats. In both cases much sake was drunk, but the results were different. A drunken soldier in the spring had been filled with laughter and might have good-humoredly thrown a copper mon to a begging child. Now a child would be wise to stay far away, for he would be more liable to receive a kick for his trouble than a coin.

The house looked deserted. I hid behind some bushes and watched but soon grew restless. As I was just about to leave, the door opened and the girl came out. She stretched herself as if she had just woken and sat down on the steps that led to the house. The roof looked even more weatherworn than when last I had seen it. A boy came out. I did not recognize him, though he might have been there when Nezumi had put his knife to my throat. Instinctively, I touched my neck. It was almost as if I could feel the weapon bruising my skin again, and I wished I had not come. The two were talking, but I was too far away to hear what they were saying. The girl got up abruptly. She sounded angry. "Why should we bother?" she shouted and stamped her foot. The boy shrugged his shoulders and said something in too low a tone for me to catch it. I leaned forward in order to hear better and broke a branch. The boy turned his head and frowned in my direction. I prepared to run for my life if he discovered me. The door slid open once more. This time it was Nezumi who came out. He spoke to the girl and the boy. He seemed to be in very good humor. The boy laughed at whatever it was he had said, and Nezumi sat down beside him. I was just about to retreat when a hand came down over my mouth and I was dragged unceremoniously from my hiding place. To my relief, it was not one of Nezumi's gang that had caught me. It was a Samurai, a young man in his early twenties.

"Do you belong to them?" The Samurai pointed toward the trees that hid the house.

I shook my head, too frightened even to speak after the rough treatment I had received.

"What were you doing, spying on them? Do you belong to another gang of thieves?"

"No, I am not a thief," I stammered, wondering if I should try and run. "I have no mother or father. My father was killed at Mikata-ga-hara."

"You are not only a thief but a liar, too." The young Samurai looked contemptuously at me. "Did your father or your mother tell you to say that?"

"It is true! They say he was killed by a spear or an arrow in the chest, and my mother died when I was born."

"It is a good story, and it might bring tears to a woman's eyes." The Samurai shook his head. "But I have heard too many similar tales to believe it."

"Did not those who died in that battle have children?" I asked. I was kneeling in front of the young warrior, looking up into his face. "I do not mind lying, I often do. But what I told you is the truth."

The young man smiled. "It may very well be, but that does not mean that you are not a thief."

I told him where I lived and that I helped the priest in the temple. He nodded several times as if saying to himself,

"Now that was a clever lie, that was a good one." But when I had finished he said: "Run along then to your temple and say your prayers to Amida Buddha. But if I am wrong in letting you go and you have long fingers, keep them to yourself for a while at least, or you will end up staring at nothing."

"My Lord, I am not a thief." I got up and bowed three times, then turned and walked away. I did not run until I was sure the Samurai could no longer see me. I was out of breath when I arrived at the temple. I could hear the priest praying, so I did not go inside but looked for my cat.

16 *Nezumi Is Dead*

As I was falling asleep that night, the girl kept appearing to me just at the moment when my eyes would close. Then I would wake again, thinking about her. I could hear Neko breathing. The cat was sleeping very close to me. "She would have killed him," I said to myself and pulled my covers over my head. But, like a ghost, the girl would return even in the darkness under my bedding. "Tomorrow," I said, "I shall go and warn her." When I had made that promise I fell asleep and did not wake before the sun had long risen.

As soon as I woke I remembered my promise. The young Samurai had as much as told me that he and his comrades were going to catch Nezumi and his gang. I will warn them, and then maybe they will leave me alone, I thought. I had no use for them, yet in a way I felt closer to them than I could possibly feel toward the young Samurai. For better or for worse, they belonged to my world. Instinctively I knew that if their story was told it would not be much different from mine.

I hid in the same place as I had the day before. The house looked no different, yet somehow I felt it was deserted. They have taken them already, I thought to myself, or maybe they have been warned and have gone. Still I waited. I watched a beetle climb up a branch of the bush I was hiding behind. "Why is it doing that?" I wondered. "There is nothing at the end of the branch that could possibly be of use to it." The beetle had almost reached the tip when it came to the same conclusion and started down again. "I am like that beetle," I thought. "Half the time I don't know where I am going and hardly ever why."

As the sun rose high in the sky, I broke from my cover and, as ready as a bird to fly, cautiously made my way toward the house. From my hiding place I had not been able to see the door. Now, to my surprise, I found that it was open. "Is it a trap?" I wondered, edging a little closer, ready to run if something moved. But nothing did, or almost nothing, for a large butterfly flew out the opening, its brilliant colors lit by the sun. "There is no one here," I thought, and went as far as the two steps leading up to the house. I heard no human sounds, only the humming of insects.

"Is there anybody here?" I said just loud enough to be heard if there were someone inside. No one answered, so I mounted the steps and called the same question once more. No answer came, and I edged slowly toward the doorway.

"It is me, Saru," I said as I entered. Some flies were buzzing around a spot on the floor. When I approached, they flew away. It is blood, I realized, as I knelt down to have a closer look. I heard a sound behind me. It was the girl, standing in the doorway.

"It is his blood. They killed him. Now you and your cat are safe," she said, and sniffed as if she were about to cry.

"What about the others?" I asked and got up.

"They took them away." The girl shivered in the summer heat.

"And how did you escape?"

"The Samurai who led them told me to run away, but I didn't. I watched it all." The girl turned and walked outside as if she could not bear to look at the bloodstained floor.

"I came to warn you," I said, following her. "He was here yesterday—the young Samurai—spying on the house. He caught me but did not hurt me."

"He killed Nezumi," the girl cried. "I hate him."

I said nothing but sat down on the steps. I had no use for the rat. He would have killed me and forgotten that he had done it a moment later.

"His father was a high-ranking Samurai."

"Whose father?" I asked, for I was not certain whom she meant.

"Nezumi. He told me. His father was executed by Lord Takeda, and all their property taken. That is why he became a robber. He wanted to avenge his father."

"Who was he? His father, I mean." I asked.

"He wouldn't tell me. That is why he called himself Nezumi. He said that his real name was sacred to him."

I felt like saying that he was probably a great liar, but I remembered that I was the monkey who listened, not the one who spoke. I nodded, pretending I believed her tale.

"I loved him," she said and then repeated the statement to convince me.

"He would have killed me," I uttered, not looking at her.

"And why shouldn't he? You came with the cripple. I

hated him. He was never a soldier. He was filled with lies."

"That is true. I did not like him either but, still, to kill him . . ." I looked up at the girl.

"Sometimes you have to kill," she said as she sat down on the top step. "Nezumi was not frightened of killing if he had to. He was no coward."

"Coward." To many there was no worse word. "Thief" or even "murderer" was preferable. I thought of telling her that I was a coward, but she would not have understood.

"Why did they have to kill him?" she wailed and looked at me as if I could answer that question.

I shrugged my shoulders. In truth, I could have answered, but she would not have liked my answer. He was killed as a mosquito is when it bites you. She is a foolish girl, I thought, yet I was pleased that the young Samurai had pitied her and let her go.

"I hope he gets killed, too." The girl kicked with her feet.

I knew she meant the young Samurai. "How many were there?" I asked.

"Too many. But Nezumi fought them. He had a sword." She added with pride, "I loved him."

I nodded again, even though I could not understand her. Nezumi was not worth loving. I think she sensed my feelings because she looked scornfully at me and said, "You would not understand. You are too young. You are only a child."

"Where are you going now?" I asked. When she frowned in reply, I said, "You can't stay here."

"Why not?" She looked at me angrily as if I had forbidden her to stay. "I will stay here if I feel like it."

"They may come back. Usually they tear down a house if

it has sheltered robbers. Or, if there are no other houses near it, they may burn it."

"Why?" She looked at me in surprise.

"If you destroy the nest, the birds fly away," I said. It was something I had heard once.

"I can go home." She frowned at the thought.

"Home!" I echoed. "Where is that?"

She mentioned the village near the three Jizo statues where I had rested. She, I thought, had known about the inn and may also have told them it would be worth robbing. "I never had a home," I said bitterly.

"I don't like my mother, and my father does not care about me." She looked down at her feet, rubbing one against the other. "I have two brothers, and there is hardly food enough. They came and took most of our rice for new taxes."

I knew that some of the peasants had left their land because they had been taxed so heavily that there was not enough left to feed them. It was the war, for an army eats but does not reap. Again, this was something I had heard. "I think it best that you go home," I said in a low voice so as not to offend. If she had been parentless like myself, I would have suggested that she come to the temple. I was glad that she wasn't, for I did not really like her.

"I didn't hurt your cat," she said and smiled at me.

"Would you have?" I asked and got up.

"I don't know." She wrinkled her forehead thoughtfully and laughed. "I don't think I could have. Nezumi wanted both you and Shiro killed as traitors. But I said you were not since you were not part of the gang. So then I suggested that I should kill your cat."

"But Nezumi did not kill Shiro?"

"Neither him nor your cat." For a moment she turned and looked through the open door into the hut where she had lived. "They hated each other, Shiro and him. One or the other of them would have had to die. And it was Nezumi. Shiro liked you."

I shook my head and mumbled, "No, he didn't like me." Then a little louder I said, "But I liked him."

The girl nodded as if she understood what I meant, that she, too, was familiar with the hurt of liking someone who did not care for her. Then she picked up a little pebble and flung it through the door of the house. "Good-bye," she said. As she walked away she turned her head and added, "I am glad I didn't hurt your cat." I watched her until she disappeared behind some trees farther down the road. I picked up a stone and threw it but missed the door and hit the wall of the house instead. The stone bounced back and fell on the ground. As I walked away I thought, "Maybe it is worse to have parents who do not care for you than not to have parents at all."

I told the priest what had happened and that the girl had been spared.

"The Samurai who led the soldiers was young, you said?" the priest asked.

"If he was the same as the one who caught me, then he has not worn his swords long."

"He could have been their older brother," the priest said and shook his head.

"No, he could not. He was a Samurai, a lord. Someone

you and I must bow to. They were only thieves." What the priest had said made me angry. Recalling the young man, I added: "But he was kinder than most Samurais."

"Saru, little monkey, you hate too much," the priest rebuked me with a smile.

"I don't," I said. "I don't hate them, but I don't like them either. If I were a Samurai's son instead of what I am, I would probably strut about like they do. They killed Nezumi and will kill the rest of the little thieves as well. But what was Nezumi but a boy playing Samurai? They killed him for being like them. I am only a monkey. I am not like them, nor do I pretend to be. All I know about them is that they killed my father and left me all alone."

"Poor Saru. Your father was killed by Takeda Shingen's enemies." The priest stroked my head in an attempt to calm me.

"If Lord Takeda had had no enemies, my father would still be alive," I said bitterly. Looking up at the priest and noticing that his eyes were wet, I cried: "I don't know . . . I am only a child!" Then, as I ran, I thought I heard the priest call after me. I did not come back to the temple before it had grown dark. I did not understand why I had become so angry, angry at the priest as well, who had only been kind to me.

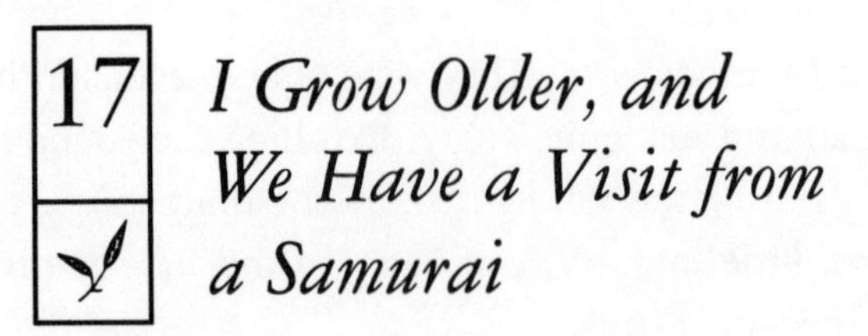

17 I Grow Older, and We Have a Visit from a Samurai

A few weeks later I went back to the house of the thieves. It was no longer there. Someone had set fire to it, and the leaves on the trees growing close to it were singed. It seemed a pity. I poked in the ashes with a stick. It had not rained since the fire, and the ashes were dry and rose in little clouds into the air. "I would have warned you," I said, as if the spirit of Nezumi was there to hear me. "Now you are gone, no longer good or bad, just forgotten. Soon winter will come. The snow will fall, and when spring comes grass will grow where the house was." I don't know why I said these things and even less why I felt that my words made me sad. "Good-bye," I said and threw a small stone onto the place where the house had once stood. It fell soundlessly into the ashes and disappeared.

I looked for the young Samurai but did not see him again. I wonder what I would have done if I had. Would I have spoken to him and asked him why he had saved the girl and why he had set fire to the house? I probably would not, but maybe I would have appealed to him, whined in my beggar's voice, "My father died at Mikata-ga-hara," to find out if he remembered me.

Winter came early that year. The first snow fell in the tenth month. I would not have survived if I had had to live in my little shrine. The shed I slept in was dry, and I had plenty of coverings. I got food every day from the priest, the very same food that he ate and sometimes even the bigger portion. "You are young, Saru. You have to grow tall like a tree, but a priest of Buddha should not grow fat, so eat, my child, eat."

Children grow and time passes; weeks become months and months years. Much of what happens to us we forget, but some things time cannot erase. I have told you about my encounter with Nezumi and his band of thieves. Should I close my eyes I would still be able to see his face in front of me. Neko, my cat, died two years after I came to the temple to live. I buried him close to the little shrine of Oinari-sama where we had spent the winter together. Sometimes when I wake in the middle of the night I think I can hear him purring close to me, then I smile and go back to sleep. I wonder if I would have survived to see the plum trees burst into blossom if Neko had not been there.

Though the next few years were hard on the people of Kai, I did not suffer. The priest treated me kindlier than most fathers treat their sons. He taught me to read the sutras and to write, and I grew so skillful that I copied sutras and sold them. I should now like to write that I grew tall and strong, but I didn't. Agile I was and I could run fast as well as climb a tree, but small I stayed. Maybe that was fitting for someone who had no other name but Saru, monkey. The priest wanted to give me another name, but I didn't want one. He laughed when I explained why. "I am used to being called Saru. It seems to me that it fits me," I said. "If I some day become somebody else, I mean, feel as if I was no longer Saru, then I will be glad to change it and get another name that suits me better."

"It would be a strange world where everyone had names that fitted them," he said. "My name was Matzuzo before I changed it when I became a priest. I took the name Jogen, or, rather, the priest who was my teacher gave me that name. But it is much too grand a name for a person like me. I should be called 'he who is quick to stumble,' or something like that." Then he laughed. "Saru, you shall be the first monkey to become a priest," he declared and shook his head.

I had no desire to become a priest, nor did I dream of becoming a Samurai. I did not think about the future but took each day as it came without wondering what the next one would bring. Our province of Kai was in turmoil. Takeda Katsuyori still ruled, was still our lord whose word was law. But no one believed that he could win. After his defeat at Takatenjin he was doomed. That was the fourteenth winter of my life. Some years of peace had been given me, when the fire and flames of the world did not touch me, but now that was over. Our Lord Katsuyori was about to fall, and no Takeda would ever rule Kai again. In his fall many would die with him and many would lose what little they had. When a mighty lord falls, the Samurais who serve him become masterless Ronins unless they can find another lord to serve. But it is not only the Samurais who lose their master when a great ruler is destroyed. For every Samurai that becomes a Ronin, a dozen ordinary lowly people are thrown out to fend for themselves or to starve. The Ronin has his pride, the swords in his obi. Poor and wretched though he may be, he can still command respect. The elderly servants of the lord's castle or the Samurai's house become beggars when their master is destroyed.

For Jogen the priest and myself, it started when the Samurai came to visit. He was young, not yet in his thirtieth year. He claimed he came to pray, though I think that was only an excuse. The priest offered him tea, and I served them. I liked him from the start. He did not have the usual arrogance of the Samurai. He was polite not only to the priest but to me as well. This was unusual, for most Samurais show their superiority by not noticing those who serve them and if they do acknowledge them it is usually to curse or kick them. This young man was different. He spoke softly and well, weighing each word as he pronounced it.

"I have passed your little temple many a time and often thought of coming in. But I am not a man who believes much in prayers." The young Samurai smiled at my friend, the priest.

"There is not one but many roads to Buddha. People who pray are like children who make demands of their parents. I pray only for one thing: to understand."

"To understand." The Samurai echoed the priest's words.

"Yes, that is worth asking for. But will understanding bring peace?"

"Without it there can be none, that is certain." The priest smiled. "A man who has the power of speech cannot claim to be dumb nor a man who has sight call himself blind. Just so, if we can think, we must try to understand. Buddha understands everything; that is why he is Buddha and, understanding everything, he has found or become peace."

The Samurai laughed. "Is this youngster your pupil?" he asked and pointed to where I was kneeling in a corner of the room listening.

"I have no pupil, no follower. To have such you have to feel sure of the way. I am more like one who is lost himself. As I said, there are many roads, and I would not be sure which is the right one. I can be no one's guide, lost in the wilderness as I am. His name is Saru, he is"—Jogen looked at me and then said—"a friend."

"Saru, that is not a name. Has he no other?" The Samurai frowned, as if the priest had told a joke which was not to his liking.

"His parents died before they could tell him, or he could understand, what his name was. People called him Saru, the little monkey. I have suggested that we find another name for him, but he says he does not want it."

"He is not the first who has been called after an animal. I knew a general who was called the Wild Bull. But that was more of a compliment. Why do you choose to be called monkey?" The Samurai looked at me and waited for me to answer.

"My Lord," I said, thinking it best to show respect, "your

general was probably like a wild bull or thought he was, and therefore the name pleased him. I am like one of the monkeys, the one who hears but seldom speaks."

"See no evil, hear no evil, and speak no evil." The Samurai drank the last of his tea and got up. "I see nothing but evil and hear only that as well. Ours is a world where the snake is the lord that rules." He bowed to the priest and then bent his head slightly toward me. When he had left, the priest said, "He came, Saru, to speak, for where he is he cannot speak. He is a man searching for truth. I hope that some day he will find it."

"He is a Samurai, and his two swords are sharp for killing. The soul of a Samurai is the blade of his sword. I do not care for such a soul," I said disdainfully.

"Saru, you judge too hastily and too harshly." The priest shook his head. "He was a man in pain."

"So he was," I agreed. "I liked him better than most of the Samurais, not that I have known many." I thought of the young Samurai I had met long ago near Nezumi's hut. "He will be back," I said knowingly and gathered up the teacups and went to wash them.

He returned only a few days later and entered the priest's room as if he were an invited guest. Again I made tea and served it. Someone had given us some chestnut cakes. I put them on a little plate and offered them to him.

"I have not tasted a cake like this for years. I thought no one made cakes anymore. Cakes belong to peace, not to war." The Samurai smiled. "My only memory of my childhood is cakes like this. There must have been chestnut trees in our garden."

"You lost your parents when you were very young?" Jogen asked. He, too, was eating a cake.

"So young that I have no memories of them . . . no, that is not completely true, I can remember the smell of my mother, the perfume she used, but what my parents looked like I would not know. War robbed me of my parents, as it stole their lives. In our times it is a story so common that it is hardly worth repeating. Saru here lost his parents as well. How did that come about?"

"As you say, My Lord, it is a tale so common it is not worth telling. My father died in the battle of Mikata-ga-hara."

"Yes, that was the beginning of the end. And your mother?"

"I killed her. Not that I wanted to, but it seems that in giving life to me she had to lose her own. I was brought up by a woman called Aya-san who died in a fire when I was very young."

"Saru used to live with his cat under the little shrine to Oinari-sama nearby." The priest grinned as a sudden thought occurred to him. "I think he might be a foster child of the little fox god."

"As a child of the gods he can probably change himself into any shape he wants to. Maybe he is not a monkey but a fox masquerading as a boy." The young man laughed and held out his cup as I offered him more tea.

"No, he is a boy and a very clever one. I have taught him to read and to write as well. He holds his brush as neatly as anyone and never does a drop of ink fall from it unless he desires it."

"A master of calligraphy. I once knew a man who was that. He was a good man." The young Samurai frowned as if his words had brought him unpleasant thoughts. He rose suddenly, bowed to the priest, and, nodding to me, he said, "It is far better to be skilled with the brush than with the sword." Then he left us. I watched him striding away. When the priest asked me if I still hated him, I shook my head. Somehow I felt sorry for him, a feeling I never expected to have for a Samurai.

18 *The Samurai Comes Again*

"Tell me, what sect does our temple belong to?" I asked the priest one day. Since the followers of Buddha seldom agree upon matters of religion, Buddhism contains many sects, each of which proclaims to know the true path to Nirvana.

The priest scratched his head and his nose, then said, "Saru, I am not too sure. The priest who was here when I came claimed he belonged to the Jodo sect but, in truth, he worshipped only money. He was a miser and would half starve himself and do worse to me and the servant he kept. He sold everything that was given to the temple. We never tasted rice or a sweet yam all the time he was here. The family who built this temple and supported it no longer exist, at least not in Kai. The last of them was that Lord Obu who revolted against Lord Takeda Shingen and lost his life because of it. When that happened the priest who was here collected everything he owned and loaded it on a horse and ran away. Like most misers, he was scared of losing his life. He expected Lord Takeda to come and kill him as he had killed his master. Nothing happened. I think Lord Shingen had other things to concern him than a poor temple like ours. So I became priest here. They say that the old priest has let his hair grow and now keeps a tavern somewhere down by the coast. I wouldn't know, but I was glad to see his heels and would be sorry to see his toes." Priest Jogen laughed and took out a handkerchief to blow his nose.

"Then we belong to the Jodo sect." I wasn't too sure exactly what that meant. Some sects can't eat meat, and others don't.

"I am not sure, Saru. Some days I think that one sect is right, that they have the map which will lead you straight to Buddha. But then I have my doubts. From Kofuchu to Kyoto, there is one road that is right. That anyone can understand, but the road to Buddha, that is something else, a matter much more complex. There could be many roads, and they could all be right. My road, Saru, and your road may not be the same, yet they may both be right."

"Then what sect do we belong to?" I asked, a little confused.

"I guess to none of them, Saru. Or maybe we belong to all of them. I am a poor priest, Saru. A priest should be like a guide who knows his country. He should be able to say something like this: 'Take that road, when you come to the river, cross it, and then take the path to the left and the first one after that to the right and when you come to the mountain, climb it and on top of it you will find Buddha.' But I am a poor guide, always in doubt of what road to take. Sometimes I think I shouldn't be a priest at all."

"I think it is much better not to belong to a sect at all," I said. "Maybe those priests who know the right road don't know it all, they only imagine that they know it. Maybe the road that they tell you to follow won't lead you to Buddha at all."

"Maybe each man has to find his own way." The priest smiled. "Maybe, Saru, it is the searching which enables you to get to Buddha. Maybe no one can tell anyone how to get to Buddha." Then he laughed. "But you, Saru, are a follower of Oinari-sama. You do not want to become a Buddha—you want to become a fox."

"Oinari-sama is the god of rice, and if you have often gone hungry he is not a bad god to have!" I, too, laughed. Then, more seriously, I said: "I have never asked help from Buddha. Oinari and stone Jizos have fitted me. Somehow I always felt that Buddha belonged to those who have clothes of silk."

"Buddha belongs to those who search for him." Priest Jogen looked solemn. "That is the only thing that I am sure of. Everything else is like a man's thoughts: little fluffy clouds in the sky which might disappear any moment."

"I don't search for Buddha. I am more like my cat, Neko, was. When the sun is in the sky I lie in its warmth and purr. To live is enough for me," I declared.

"You are a monkey." At that moment someone knocked on the door. I went and slid it open. It was the Samurai. He greeted us and then sat down on the floor. I went to fetch tea for him. When I returned, he was sitting silently staring out in front of him. Priest Jogen was silent, too. Both of them looked as if they were meditating. We had heard strange rumors of what went on in Tsutsujigasaki Castle, the residence of the Takeda family. It had not sounded pleasant. But what we had listened to had been servants' gossip, for no Samurai came to worship at our little temple.

The Samurai acknowledged the tea with a nod. The priest mumbled a thank-you. I joined them, and we sat like three stone Jizos for a while. Finally the young Samurai said: "He is mad." He shook his head and was silent once more.

I wanted to ask, "Who is mad?" but I didn't dare.

"He has not been used to losing. To lose and learn from your loss is a gift that has to be acquired," Priest Jogen suggested. I understood that the Samurai was referring to our master, the lord of Kai, Takeda Katsuyori.

"He is mad." The Samurai repeated. To my surprise I saw that a tear had formed in his eye and was now running down his cheek.

"We have heard evil news from the castle but did not know if it was the truth." The priest turned his teacup around and around. "We had hoped it was merely servants' gossip."

"Evil it is to kill the wives and children of those who once were your friends. Even the old are not sacred. This morning the mother of someone who has fled the castle was killed."

"He had betrayed Katsuyori?" The priest lifted his teacup to drink but, finding it empty, set it down again.

"I think that Katsuyori has betrayed us all. But he should not have fled, knowing what would happen to his mother if he did."

"And you?" The priest held out his cup as I poured more tea. "Have you someone in the castle as well?"

"A wife." The Samurai looked around the room, as if surprised to find himself there. "I have not seen her for several weeks." I offered him more tea, and he thanked me.

"Can you not go and see her?" the priest asked.

"Katsuyori keeps his hostages in one part of the castle and allows no one near them. I have had notes from her. She is alive and says she is well." Then the Samurai smiled as if he recalled something pleasant. "Once before we exchanged letters, but that was long ago."

"He does not trust you?" Priest Jogen asked.

"Katsuyori does not trust anyone anymore. He feels that he has been betrayed by all. The truth is that Katsuyori betrayed Katsuyori, no one else did. That is at least until recently. But can you blame anyone for not wanting to die for someone whom he now despises? Those who are loyal are loyal because of the love they had for his father."

"Yes, Takeda Shingen was much respected." Again the priest started turning his cup around and around.

"He was worthy of it, as was my master." The Samurai made a grimace. "His one error was that he killed the wrong son."

"Who was your master?" I asked. Both the priest and the Samurai looked at me in surprise. A youth does not speak unless he is spoken to.

For a moment I thought the Samurai was going to reprimand me, but he said, "Lord Akiyama Nobutomo."

"Was he a very old man?" I asked.

"He was a man in the prime of his life when he died. Why do you ask that?"

"Once a very old man, a Lord Akiyama, sent for me. I think he said he had a son. He wanted me to deliver a message for him. I did so, and he gave me a silver coin. He was kind, but I did not like his servants."

"That was my lord's father. He is still alive but very old and weak now. The death of his son aged him. Who was the message for?"

"Someone who lives down by the river. He had gone soldiering and is dead now. I think the old lord wanted him to deliver a message to his son."

The Samurai smiled. "He told me about you. He even remembered that you were called Saru. He often wondered why you did not come back."

I shrugged my shoulders. I was not sure why I had not gone back. It had been only partly because of the servants.

"I didn't belong there," I said, though that did not really explain anything. "The servant was very rude to me and his son tried to steal my money, but I was too quick for him."

"They have both gone. They took along a good many things which did not belong to them. If I ever find them, they shan't steal from anyone ever again."

He rose and bowed in his usual manner, first to Priest Jogen and then to me. As he slid open the door he turned toward me and said: "Who knows where any of us belong? I thought I knew, but now I am not sure anymore."

When the Samurai closed the door and his footsteps had died away, the priest said, "He is suffering. He is in the raging fire of the world; we are not, Saru. Rinse the teacups, and then go and lie in the sunshine and purr."

I picked up the cups. I wanted to protest that I, too, had been burned by that raging fire of the world mentioned in one of the prayers to Buddha. But I decided not to. I just cleaned the cups and kettle and put everything away.

19 *The Girl Nami*

I had never gone near Tsutsujigasaki Castle. I had seen it at a distance, for it is situated in the outskirts of the city of Kofuchu. The day after the visit from the Samurai I decided to go there. The castle covers a large area. It has tall ramparts and a moat around it. It seemed to me impregnable. I wondered how deep the water was in the moat. As I leaned out, I could see fat carp swimming. Someone shouted from the rampart. I looked up and saw a soldier fitting an arrow to his bow and pointing it in my direction. I stood up but didn't run away. I wondered if he would shoot me. I was not the least bit scared, although I had no wish to die.

"Don't shoot!" a voice shouted near me. I turned around in surprise. It was a girl a little younger than myself. She grabbed me by the arm and pulled me away. I followed her, glancing back at the soldier. He had lowered his bow.

"Do you want to get killed?" she asked when we were a distance from the castle.

I shook my head. "Would he have killed me?"

"Yes," she said, "they have orders to shoot anyone who comes near the moat."

"Why?" I asked and sat down on the ground underneath a tree. "I had no weapon."

"It is an order," the girl replied as if that were an answer in itself.

"How do you know?" I asked, looking at the girl. She had seated herself cross-legged beside me. Her bare feet were dirty, but her clothes, though far from new, were clean.

"I live there." She nodded toward the castle. "My father is the head cook. He is a very important man. All the soldiers know me."

I grinned and said, "No wonder you are fat with a father who is a cook." For some reason I had never thought there would be children living inside the castle. Foolishly I had populated it only with Samurais.

"I am not fat. I have a round face and I am very pretty, so my mother says. What does your father do and where do you live?"

"My father is a very important person," I teased. "And we live in a castle."

"Your father keeps pigs and you live in a pigsty," she replied and laughed.

"That is true. I was born in the year of the boar. So was my father. That is why the pigs like us. I bet you were born in the year of the horse."

"I was not. I was born in the year of the snake. What does your father really do? Do you have a farm?"

"My father died in the battle of Mikata-ga-hara. I live in a temple to Buddha and serve the priest. I do most of the cooking, so I am a cook, too."

"Is your mother dead, too?" the girl asked.

"She died when I was born."

"You are lucky. My mother hates me. She only likes my brother. He always gets the best and is never asked to do anything. I hate my mother."

"Why not hate your brother instead?" I could not help asking.

"It is not his fault; besides he is younger than me. You can't really hate anyone younger than yourself."

I nodded in agreement. "Can you go anywhere you want to inside the castle?"

"Almost anywhere," she boasted.

"What is your name?" I demanded. "Mine is Saru."

"Monkey." She laughed. "Mine is Nami."

"Nami . . . it is a pretty name. But we are far from the sea, so why were you called wave? There are waves only on the ocean."

"My father called me that because he was born by the sea. His father was a fisherman. He says the sea is very beautiful and that the waves are like girls with long white hair."

I laughed. "But your hair is black so you won't be a proper Nami, wave, before you are a grandmother."

"You are a stupid boy. Monkey is the right name for you."

"I am sorry. I do think Nami is a very nice name." I smiled to let her know that I meant it.

"Have you ever been by the sea?" she asked in a serious tone.

"I have been no farther than a few ri from Kofuchu. The sea is very, very far away, maybe a hundred ri or more. I would like to see it." Suddenly, though I had never thought about it before, I said, "Some day I will go there and see if all the little waves are pretty like you."

"I am not really pretty." Nami rubbed one big toe against the other. "In the castle there are ladies who are very beautiful, and they wear silk kimonos. One has embroidered butterflies and another cranes. Sometimes I dream that I have become a lady like that and am married to a handsome Samurai." She smiled dreamily, seeing herself dressed in silk. Then her expression changed. "But that won't ever, ever happen."

"I think that some of the ladies in silk might be happy to change places with you, if what I have heard is true. They say that some of them have been killed."

"Only those whose husbands have betrayed our lord. Katsuyori-sama gets very angry when they betray him."

"But they haven't betrayed him. Only their husbands have," I argued.

"Whatever your husband does, you have done. So if he betrays his lord, you have betrayed him as well." Nami looked solemnly at me. "Isn't that true?"

"I am a monkey, so I don't have a master." I thought that what she had just said was something a grownup had told her. "But I don't see why he should kill women who have not betrayed him and children, too."

"He!" Nami looked shocked. "Katsuyori-sama is not he. You are he! Takeda Katsuyori-sama is our lord, to whom we must be loyal."

"Katsuyori is no lord of mine." The words escaped me

and shocked me. "I serve no lord!" I almost shouted, and then more softly I whispered, "I am a monkey and monkeys have no lords."

"If Katsuyori-sama heard you talk like that he would have your head cut off. Then you would be a headless monkey." Nami laughed.

"Do you know—" Suddenly I realized that I did not know the name of the Samurai who came to visit us in the temple. I was about to ask Nami if she knew his wife.

"Do I know what?" Nami asked.

"Nothing . . . it is of no importance. I was going to ask you about someone in the castle, but I don't know his name."

"There are no monkeys in the castle, they live up in the hills." Nami pointed to the mountains that rose beyond the castle.

For the first time I was tired of my name and wished I had another. "He is not a monkey. He is a Samurai and wears two swords." I conjured up an image of him in my mind as I spoke. "He comes to worship at our temple and drinks tea with my master and myself."

"Is your temple very big?" Nami asked.

For a moment I was tempted to lie and tell her that it was, but I thought better of it. "It is very small," I admitted, "and no one of importance worships there. Old grandfathers and grandmothers come because they have worshipped there since they were young. Its patron used to be Lord Obu, who was killed by Lord Takeda Shingen."

"Then you are poor, your master and you." Disarmed by

my honesty, Nami said, "It is not true that my father is head cook. He is only a cook's helper. But it is true that most of the soldiers know me."

I nodded in acknowledgment. Most children lie and brag about their parents. It is only natural. "That Samurai has a wife in the castle, and he is not allowed to see her. He is very sad. Most of the time he just sits and stares in front of him, as if seeing something which my master and I can't see. I feel very sorry for him."

"If he does not betray Lord Takeda then he has nothing to feel sad about." Nami looked toward the gateway of the castle. A man on horseback was approaching. "If he is not allowed to see his wife, I think that Katsuyori-sama does not trust him."

"That may be." I, too, watched the rider. He dismounted, and a servant held the bridle of his horse. "A messenger bringing news from somewhere," I thought.

"I must go back or my mother will get angry." Nami stood up.

"Do you often come here?" I asked. Not only did I like the girl, but I also thought that friendship with her might be useful.

"Sometimes I like to get outside the castle. If I come it is usually in the morning." Nami smiled shyly.

"Good," I said, as if we had agreed upon meeting again.

"Good-bye . . . Saru." Nami ran toward the gate, her little legs hitting the earth like drumsticks hitting the skin of a drum. The soldiers guarding the gate shouted something at her as she ran past them. "It is true," I thought, "the soldiers know her and like her." I sat underneath the tree and watched the castle until the sun was at its highest in the sky, when I remembered that my master would be hungry.

When I told him about the girl I had met, he laughed. "Another monkey. All children are monkeys, but some day they have to grow into human beings."

"Then they don't climb trees anymore but cut the heads off each other instead. I shall stay a monkey," I replied.

20 *Murakami Harutomo*

"If he kills my wife, I shall kill him." The Samurai looked first at my master, Priest Jogen, and then at me. "Her father was killed by Oda Nobunaga when my lord died. She would have died, too, had not my servant saved her. Lord Oda also likes to cut off heads. When my master, Lord Akiyama, lost Iwamura Castle, Lord Oda cut off heads until they were piled up like freshly dug radishes. He had promised my master safe conduct for him and his men if he gave up the castle. That was but a ruse. Once the gates to the castle were opened he had everyone killed."

"If Lord Takeda Katsuyori has your wife killed, he will have you killed as well." The priest spoke softly, as if such words needed to be whispered.

"If she dies it does not matter what happens to me. Maybe it does not even matter if I do not revenge her. I wanted to kill Lord Oda and revenge my master. But I couldn't. When I was a child I had only one dream: to be a Samurai and wear the two swords. Now . . ." The Samurai shook his head sadly and said no more.

"Why does Lord Takeda not trust you?" the priest asked.

The Samurai sighed. "Oh, he has good reasons. My master, Lord Akiyama, belonged to those captains who suggested that after Katsuyori's father, Lord Shingen, died, Kai should be ruled by a council of the older captains. Katsuyori's son, Nobukatsu, who was a mere child, was to be named lord and ruler of Kai. Takeda Katsuyori never forgave those men. Most of them died in the battle of Nagashino. At a council meeting, the only one I was ever allowed to attend, held after that defeat, I suggested that he should retire as our lord and allow his son to have his position. I guarded my tongue carefully when I spoke, even hinting that he would retain power after he retired just as retired emperors are still emperors. Although there were many at the meeting who agreed with me, not one of them spoke up. Katsuyori's face was white as snow. Then two red roses bloomed on his cheeks. After that my wife was kept from me."

"No, he will not trust you again, I see that," Priest Jogen sighed.

"Oh, he never did trust me. Katsuyori likes only those who agree with him and praise even his most foolish thoughts. Why, he cannot even compose a poem which is not an insult to that art. His father and his father's brother were both good poets."

Priest Jogen smiled. "You write poetry yourself?" he asked, indicating to me that more tea was needed.

"I did once." The Samurai looked almost embarrassed. "Sometimes I think I would like to do it again and I write a poem in my mind. But I do not waste paper or ink on them."

"Saru here"—the priest smiled at me as I poured

tea—"writes a very pretty hand. He handles the brush with such ease that given time he may become a master."

"And does he write poetry, too?" The Samurai looked at me as if he had not noticed me before.

I shook my head. "I have never written poetry. I copy sutras and sell them to whoever wishes to buy them. If I did try, I fear it would be even more foolish than Lord Katsuyori's efforts." I said this because I had sensed a note of irony in the Samurai's tone.

"I am sure that the elegance of your letters would not be betrayed by the sense they were conveying." The Samurai lifted one hand in a slight, graceful movement toward me.

This time I felt he was sincere and replied, "I have never thought about writing a poem. When I saw the sun setting upon the first snow fallen on the mountains and painting them red as blood, I thought it pretty. But I did not think about describing it in words."

"Maybe it is but a foolish pastime of those whose hands are too idle. Yet it gave me pleasure." With a smile that enhanced his features and made him handsome, he said, "No, that is not true. It is not foolish. To be able to describe a feeling or a thought in a few spare words is the noblest of arts. A poem is the kernel of thought or a feeling." The Samurai blushed as if ashamed of the passion with which he had spoken.

I nodded to show that I had understood him. From that moment on I truly liked the Samurai. I felt that I wanted to help him, even to serve him. I swore to myself that I would try and learn how to write poetry. Bowing my head a little, I said, "The kernel of a nut is the only valuable part. The shell we throw away."

"Some of the sutras, prayers to Buddha, are in themselves poems," Priest Jogen said. "Like Saru, I have never written poetry, though sometimes I have felt like it. When in despair and not knowing which way to turn, I would go for a walk to some place where I could be alone, where I could not see even the roof or the gable of a house. Then, listening to the wind in the trees, to nature breathing, I would feel better. Maybe I should have written poems instead?"

The Samurai smiled. "You are wise. Nature makes us feel small and unimportant, but it also makes our despair, our unhappiness, smaller and easier to bear. It was but yesterday that I went for a walk in the mountains for exactly that reason. But it did not help me." He paused. "My despair was not so much mine as my wife's. I see her in front of me, a living ghost who visits me at all times. If I cannot save her, then. . . ." The Samurai touched the shorter of his swords, the one used when committing seppuku, when you take your own life.

Priest Jogen shook his head. "I know you Samurais believe that it is an honorable way to end one's life. It is a custom held as heroic . . . second only to death on the battlefield. I cannot agree. You have a duty to save your wife, even to die in the attempt. But to take your own life, no. I think it is a sin to take your own life. The duty of man—and sometimes it is hard to bear—is to live."

"I know someone in the castle," I blurted out. In my mind I had already been trying to think of ways to save the Samurai's wife.

"I know a lot of people in the castle." The Samurai looked at me in annoyance. "But that is no help. None of them would endanger themselves for me or my wife's sake."

"Oh, it is no one of importance. Her father is a cook," I hastened to add, "but she says that she can go anywhere in the castle and that she knows all the soldiers."

The priest glanced quizzically at me. "Who is this young person, Saru, and when did you get to know her?"

"Only a few days ago. Her name is Nami. She told the soldier not to shoot me."

"And why should the soldier shoot you?" the priest asked with a smile.

"I was looking into the moat, watching the fat carp swimming there. They have orders to shoot anyone who approaches the moat, so Nami told me. But when she shouted, 'Don't shoot,' he lowered his bow. Then we talked for a while. She is only a big child, at least two years younger than I am."

"Maybe she could carry a message?" The Samurai looked hopefully at me.

"She could, for sure," I said. "Maybe she could do more than that. The soldiers are not always that watchful at the gate."

"If only I could get her out, we could go somewhere to the province of Echigo. My father served Uesugi Kenshin," the Samurai said eagerly.

"But Uesugi Kenshin is dead. Someone else rules Echigo now," the priest said.

"Uesugi Kagekatsu has broken faith with Takeda Katsuyori, and they are no longer friends. If I tell him that my father served his uncle, Kenshin, he may do something for me."

"He may or he may not. I think the words of such lords are not to be trusted. I know of a temple by the sea, in the garden of which nightingales sing. It is very beautiful, not that the temple is much. The salt winds have weathered its boards, and it is poor. The people who live there seldom taste rice. They are fishermen. The priest who has charge of it is kind and nearer to Buddha than most. You could go there and be safe."

"We talk as if my wife were here, seated beside me. She is not. . . ." The Samurai stood up. "But do ask your Nami if she could deliver a message for me." He was about to go when suddenly he realized that he had never told us his name. "I am called Murakami Harutomo. My wife's name is Aki-hime." He bowed and left the room, his right hand resting on the hilt of his sword.

For a while after the Samurai had left the priest and I sat silent. Then the priest said, "Saru, do you like him?"

I nodded but said nothing. Priest Jogen smiled. "I liked him, too, but be careful, for to them we are but fleas. Even monkeys can fall from trees."

"Yes," I said, recalling that I had heard that old saying once before. "I shall be careful," I said.

"There has been much killing lately. The tigers are fighting, and the ravens are growing fat. But rivers of tears have been shed as well. Best are the times when the swords stay in their scabbards. The Samurais may mirror themselves in the shiny blades of their weapons and think they are seeing their souls. But Saru, that is all vanity. I do not think anyone can walk the road to Buddha with a sword in his scarf. I have grown fond of you and your monkey tricks. I do not want to mourn you."

"I shall be careful." His words had touched me. "Yet maybe helping him to save his wife is one of the ways toward Buddha."

"Who knows, Saru, who knows? Our birth is a mystery and our lives a labyrinth we have to find our way through."

21 *Inside Tsutsujigasaki Castle*

The very next day I went to spy on the castle. I had changed my clothes and was wearing a ragged old hunting coat and a loincloth. I looked like a beggar child. Beggars are like fleas, unnoticed unless they bite. I would not be worth wasting an arrow on. A kick would suffice for the likes of me. I was careful, not going too close to the moat. When I met anyone I held out my hand. The kind people looked away, the rest either cursed or ignored me. By this time there were so many beggars in Kofuchu that few of them could scrounge enough money or food to stay alive. Some of them had been wounded in the battles that Katsuyori had fought and lost, but this helped them little in their professions as beggars. Some I had seen were but live skeletons covered by skin, and I thought that my father was lucky that he had been killed, not crippled.

I learned little. The castle looked to me impregnable. I was about to go homeward when I noticed a group of pack-horses approaching the castle gate. Two men were leading eight horses all tied together in a long line. The last of the horses suddenly stopped, putting all four feet down in a stubborn manner. The rope tying it to the horse in front grew taut and snapped. The horse turned, thinking that freedom lay in the opposite direction from the castle. It started to trot away, the rope trailing in the dust behind it. I ran out and grabbed the rope. For a moment the horse pulled me along but then stopped, turned its head sadly, and looked at me. It did not escape a whack over the rump when its master came running. It took the punishment as a matter of course. Packhorses are like beggar children—they don't expect much out of life.

"Come along, you can help us. I shall give you something for it." The soldier gave the horse another blow and left me in charge of the other end of the poor animal. In this way I entered Tsutsujigasaki Castle, the residence of the lord of Kai, Takeda Katsuyori. The soldiers at the gate did not notice me but shouted greetings to the two men in charge of the horses. The horses were led to a storehouse and there unburdened. I think it was millet they had been carrying. There were several sections to the buildings inside the ramparts. Those near the warehouse that the sacks were being carried into were obviously storehouses too. Some soldiers came to help with the unloading. I stood still, holding onto my horse. Mine was the last to lose its burdens. The soldier who had asked me to help was a rough-looking man, but when he smiled you could sense that he was not unkind. He patted the horse and grinned as he said, "So you were going to run away," and shook his head in mock sadness.

"My father was a soldier, too," I said, hoping to prolong my stay inside the castle.

"*Was*. Is he dead, boy?"

I nodded. "He died at Mikata-ga-hara."

"I suppose one battle is as good as another to die in. There is no reason to be too choosy about that. I have always held that it is better to die in a victory than in a defeat. It gives your widow something to be proud of."

"My mother is dead, too," I said, and arranged my features to look appropriately sad.

"Your wife will be lucky, not having a mother-in-law." The soldier laughed at his own joke and dug into his sleeve to see if a copper coin was hiding there. "I thought I had a couple of mons left." He grumbled, trying his other sleeve, and then shook his head sadly. What excuse he was going to make for not paying me I never found out, for at that moment I heard someone calling "Saru!" It was Nami. She came running up, greeting the soldier by name. He looked relieved at seeing her. "Do you know this monkey, Nami?" he asked.

"Sure," she said. "He lives in the trees up there." She pointed to the mountains in back of the castle. "But every once in a while he comes down here to visit me."

"As I was overcharged by the owner of the last inn we stopped at, for some sake not much better than well water, I am out of funds and can't pay your friend for his help." He smiled good-naturedly. "But if you could take him along to your father and see that he has his belly filled, that would do just as well."

"Come, Saru!" Nami commanded and started off. I bowed to the soldier and followed her, thinking that I had been lucky.

As soon as we were out of the soldier's sight, Nami

stopped and, turning to me, demanded fiercely, "What do you want? Why have you come here?"

"I wanted to see the castle," I said, looking around me as if that had indeed been the purpose of my visit.

"How did you get in? It is dangerous to come here. If you are caught, they will kill you."

I explained that it was by the accident of a broken rope that I got inside the walls.

"Are you hungry?"

I shook my head. The building we were standing by was not a storehouse. I wondered what it was and asked her.

"The guards on duty sleep there. Most of the soldiers live outside the castle. It is only when they are on duty that they are here."

"But what if the enemy comes? I mean, there wouldn't be any soldiers then."

"What a foolish thing to say. If we were attacked then all the soldiers would be inside the castle, as would all the Samurais that live in Kofuchu. But this castle is not safe, so Lord Katsuyori is having another one built, and we shall all be moving there." Nami talked about Lord Takeda Katsuyori as if he were an intimate friend who had asked her advice before starting to build his new castle.

"Where does Lord Katsuyori live?" I asked.

Nami nodded in the direction of a larger building, the roof of which I could just see. "He is gone. He went this morning. I saw him leave with at least a hundred Samurais on horseback. Maybe not as many as a hundred, but a lot."

I wondered if Nami could count to a hundred. I wanted to ask where the women that Katsuyori held as hostages lived but thought it unwise to mention it yet. Instead I asked, "Where do you live, Nami?"

"Oh, over there." Nami pointed vaguely at the northern corner of the castle, and I guessed that her shelter was no palace.

"What is in that building?" I continued, indicating a roof a little higher than the others.

"That is where the ladies live, the wives of high-ranking officers. They all wear nothing but silk," Nami added with a touch of wonder and envy.

"Do you go there?" I asked in a tone which I hoped sounded indifferent.

"Sometimes I am sent there. But they have their own servants." Nami looked down at her bare feet and scowled. "They are not dressed in silk, but their clothes are pretty."

I could not help smiling. What a vain little girl Nami was! "I know the name of someone there, do you know her? Her name is Aki . . . Aki-hime."

Nami shook her head. "There is one there who is very sad. She is small, tiny like a little bird and very pretty. She is married to a Samurai who is not allowed in the castle. I have never heard her name. It may be Aki, but she is no princess. She always smiles at me. The other ladies are afraid of her. One of these days I think Katsuyori will have her killed." Nami sounded as matter-of-fact as a farmer's wife talking about a hen.

"That must be her," I said. "Maybe she was a princess before she married the Samurai. Don't you feel sorry for her?"

"If her husband is a traitor to Lord Katsuyori, then I don't feel sorry." Nami was loyal, there was not much doubt of that.

"But why should she die because her husband is a traitor?" I asked.

Nami looked a little confused, as if she had never given that question a thought before. "But you have to punish traitors," she replied.

I was going to argue that because the husband is a traitor does not mean that the wife is when somebody suddenly grabbed me by the scruff of my neck and shook me.

"What are you doing here, dog?" a voice shouted. "Are you here to steal?"

"No!" I shouted, squirming to see who was holding me. It was a soldier, a bowman.

"He helped some soldiers bring in a load of millet," Nami argued. I noticed she did not call the soldier by name. He was obviously not one of the ones she knew.

"You come along to the gatehouse!" the bowman ordered.

At the castle gate we stopped. My captor demanded of the soldiers there if any of them knew me. They all took a long look at me, but none of them admitted to having seen me before. I explained what had happened, but no one believed me. The Samurai on duty at the gate was called, and I was introduced to him.

"Do you admit it?" the young Samurai asked.

"My Lord, I am no thief," I said. "I am merely a poor boy whose father was killed at Mikata-ga-hara. I came inside the castle because I helped some soldiers. They were bringing some loads of millet, and one of their packhorses broke loose and I caught it."

"The boy is good at lying." The Samurai grinned and looked at the soldiers near him. "What is the punishment for theft?" he asked.

"His head!" The soldiers laughed. I looked for Nami. She was standing a little away, her face pale as the moon.

"I wonder if my sword is sharp enough?" The Samurai drew his sword and examined it critically. Then he commanded me to bow my head.

"Monkeys do fall from trees," I said to myself. There was no escaping. I bowed my head and waited for the sword to fall. Instead of the sword, a kick in my behind sent me sprawling.

"I would not disgrace my sword by cutting off your useless head. Run, you thieving puppy, before I change my mind!"

As I ran I could hear the soldiers laughing. It had been a good joke, one that had made the young Samurai popular with his men.

22 *I Meet Shiro Again*

"I hate Samurais, I hate Samurais," I muttered to myself as I made my way back to the little temple. The words made a chant that I could keep in step with. "I hate Samurais. . . . I hate Samurais," I kept singing until I was home. Suddenly I realized that I was whole, that I hadn't lost my head, that Saru was still Saru. It made me laugh. "So you made a fool of yourself," I said. "But you are alive, and that is all that matters."

I did not tell the priest about my adventure in the castle, partly because it had been more foolish than wise, partly because it would have worried him. He might even have made me promise not to do anything like it again, and I never liked to break my word, at least not to him. I waited eagerly for the Samurai to return, but several days passed without his coming. I thought I would tell him what I had heard from Nami, even though that was hardly good news.

A few days later I was idly watching a litter being carried along the main street in Kofuchu. It was guarded by six soldiers. I decided it was some Samurai who had been to a temple to pray, not Katsuyori but some minor lord of importance, one of those you have to bend in the dust for. Just then one of the men carrying the litter caught my attention. He was young and strong, maybe three or four years older than myself. Somehow he looked familiar. The litter passed, but I ran after it and caught up with it. The soldiers kept people away from the litter, and I thought it might be one of the noble ladies that they were carrying. You cannot see who is inside. The little window has a bamboo screen and curtains. The younger of the two men carrying it saw me and grinned, then he winked. I recognized him and almost cried aloud, "Shiro!" He was the boy who had saved me when I was in the house of the band of thieves and whom I had saved later when he had been caught in the inn. He had betrayed me, I felt, yet I was not angry at him. As I ran along following the litter I suddenly realized how much I missed having a friend my own age to talk to.

It did not surprise me that they were heading for the castle. I was careful to keep far enough behind the procession so that I did not appear to be following it. I stopped a good distance from the castle but near enough to watch the guards as it entered. Whoever was inside the litter was someone of importance, possibly even Katsuyori himself. I waited a long time, hoping that Shiro would come since he had recognized me. I was far from willing to trust him, but he could tell me about life in the castle and even Katsuyori's plans. Masters often believe that they can keep secrets from their servants, but even words whispered in Tsutsujigasaki Castle, where fear reigned, sounded as loud as the conch shell does when it trumpets its commands during battle.

It was late in the afternoon, and I had almost given up all

hope when I saw Shiro approaching. He stopped by the soldiers at the gate. Laughing, he told them a joke as if they were his comrades. He looked around, searching, I thought, for me. When he saw me he gave the smallest of nods and walked away from the castle. I followed him but did not attempt to catch up before we were out of sight of the soldiers. "Shiro," I called, and he stopped. With a grin he looked me over.

"You have grown," he said.

"Not as much as you; I hardly recognized you." For a moment we stood looking at each other as if we were two strangers who had just met. Finally I asked, "How is Ojii-san?"

"Dead," Shiro answered, then added tersely, "last year, at the end of the winter."

"I liked him," I said, trying to conjure up a picture in my mind of the old man.

"He was old. He had lived a long time."

"He was good," I said. It is not tragic when a very old person dies, yet I could not help feeling that my own little world had become smaller because of his death. "Did you ever tell him that you had no uncle?" I asked.

Shiro laughed. "You have a good memory."

"Yes, I am often alone and I think of what happened then."

"Then?" Shiro mocked. "Has nothing happened to you since? Are you still renting the cellar of Oinari-sama's shrine?"

"No, I live somewhere else now. Are you a servant in the castle?"

"I am a beast of burden, no more than that." Then he added a little unhappily, "You are not tall, but you look as if you ate at least twice a day."

"I do, but surely you are well fed or you could not carry the litter. Is it very heavy?"

"They don't always remember to feed us. They are like poor farmers who starve their beasts. The litter is heavy enough to tire you. The lady I carried to the temple weighs little. She went to say prayers for her husband, and little good that will do."

"If you are hungry, I have some money." I felt in my sleeve for some copper coins. "I am hungry myself; let us go and have some soba."

I led him to the soba shop whose owner had been so kind to me when I was a beggar child. There was no one else in her little hut, but her buckwheat noodles were still the best in Kofuchu.

"Do you eat here often?" Shiro asked, making no effort to hide his envy.

"Sometimes." I shrugged my shoulders as if to add, "When I feel like it." "Would you like some sake?" I asked in order to impress him. It was a childish revenge, but I enjoyed it. The owner brought a small pitcher of sake and poured for both of us. I didn't particularly like sake but lifted my tiny cup as if I were used to drinking it. Shiro emptied his and smacked his lips as if he were an experienced judge of the quality of rice wine. Then we both laughed, and for a moment we were again friends as we had been after the "battle" in the inn.

"They have so little food that even the soldiers are hungry most of the time. You never see rice or soba either. There is a cook who cooks gruel, which is mostly ditch water seasoned with snails and dead cats. Some of the time you can hardly get it down, even though you are hungry." Shiro scowled, and when the soba came he held the bowl up to his lips and pushed the noodles into his mouth with his chopsticks as if he had not eaten for a fortnight.

"He is storing food for his army." Shiro laughed. "But his army is like a leaking tub. For every man he gets, two leave. Some time ago one of his most trusted Samurais left, together with the twenty men that served him. Only his mother remained behind, and she was as old as the hills over there." Shiro pointed at the mountains.

"What happened to her?" I asked, though I knew the answer.

"He had the old crone killed." Shiro grinned as if the death of the old lady was a subject for amusement.

"He left his own mother, knowing that she would be killed?" Perhaps because I had never known what it was like to have a mother, I was horrified at the thought. "Could he not have saved her?"

"It would have cost him a lot of silver. The old lady knew this, and she was the one who told him to leave. Katsuyori-sama should have kept his wife or children instead."

"She knew what would happen to her if her son deserted and yet she told him to leave? That was very brave of her." I poured the last of the sake into Shiro's cup.

"She claimed she was not worth even one single silver coin

to the Samurai that came to kill her. He was a young fellow and took it hard. He was as white as the moon when he had done it."

"Katsuyori would have taken the silver and let her go?" I asked. I did not add "sama" to our lord's name.

"Katsuyori-sama would not have let her go for all the gold in his father's mine."

"But you said that she could have been freed for silver?"

"Ah yes, but the silver would not have landed in Katsuyori's sleeve."

"Then if someone has silver, he can buy his wife or child free?" I asked eagerly.

"I know some who have escaped. How? No one asks. A soldier is punished, and everyone shrugs his shoulders. Gold and silver will buy anything in this world."

"Your world, Katsuyori's world," I said to myself, "but there are places where it is not true." I thought of Priest Jogen. No silver or gold could make him commit an injustice. "Would you need a lot of silver," I asked.

"Some would be more expensive than others. It depends on their husband or their father's rank." I had ordered another bowl of soba for Shiro, and he was eating it almost as eagerly as the first.

"Is there no other way they can escape?"

"If there were, Katsuyori would be all alone." Now Shiro, too, had dropped the "sama."

"Would no one stay?"

"A few would, some from loyalty to his father, Shingen, more because they fear becoming Ronins, for what is a Ronin but a two-sworded beggar or robber? They all know the end will come soon, and what then?" Shiro laughed and drew one of his chopsticks across his belly as if he were committing seppuko.

"You don't like the Samurais?" I asked, almost adding an "either."

Shiro looked at me in surprise. "Some I like, some I don't like. They are like the sun or the moon or the trees that grow on the mountains. One cannot like or dislike them. They are there, just as I am. There will always be lords, and they will be served by Samurais, who will either obey them or rebel against them. They are the spiders, you and I are the flies. All we have to learn is not to be caught in their nets."

"I suppose that is true," I said hesitatingly, "but surely we should be more than flies?"

"The flies are born in dung, and where were we born?" Shiro smiled, pleased by his own words. "Neither you nor I, or the woman whose soba we have been eating, can claim a higher birth. It is the way of the world. Maybe somewhere beyond the rim of the ocean things are different. Those strange hairy ones that have come to our shores claim it is so, but I say they are liars!" Abruptly a new thought came to him and he laughed. "Maybe you are right, we are not flies. We are eels born in the mud but difficult to catch."

"There are many worlds," I thought to myself, "but he does not know it. He does not search for the road to Buddha like Priest Jogen. For him there is only one road, and he will travel it until it ends in his death." "Do you sleep in the castle?" I asked. I wanted to hear no more about flies or eels.

"On the ground beside the litter. There are no stables for human horses." A soldier entered and nodded toward Shiro. I decided that it would be unwise to ask more questions and drew out my copper coins to pay. I had one mon left over. I offered it to Shiro, who took it without thanks and swaggered back to the castle, well satisfied with that world which had supplied him with a copper coin in his sleeve and a stomach filled with buckwheat noodles.

23 *I Tell of Shiro to Murakami-san*

"She let herself be killed to save her son." Priest Jogen nodded in approval. "There are many stories about a mother's love for her child." The priest paused for a moment and then smiled as he added, "If it is a boy; I can recall no tale when such a sacrifice is made for a daughter."

I thought of Nami and Ume and said, "Yes, it is best to be a boy."

"Not always. Remember that the Samurai who killed the little robbers let the girl go. Still, you are right; the women carry many burdens that we are spared."

"Why did the Samurai who came here not pay some money to get his wife free?" I had told the priest all that I had learned from Shiro.

"I doubt if he has much silver in his sleeve. You are still thinking about him. What does a monkey care about the fate of a Samurai?"

Though the priest was teasing me, I answered seriously. "He is the first Samurai that I have wished some luck. I would like to help him if I could."

"Many days have passed since he was last here. For all you

and I know, he may have been forced by Katsuyori to commit seppuko. But you are right in caring for him, though there might be little you and I can do to help him. So far he has only asked to borrow my ear. I have two silver coins buried in a corner of my room. He would be welcome to them, but I am afraid they would help no more than a cup of water when the house is on fire." Priest Jogen and I were sitting on the steps leading to his temple.

"What will happen to them all when Oda Nobunaga's army comes?" I asked, still thinking of the Samurai.

"I do not know. Some will die and some become Ronins. A few lucky ones may live to serve Tokugawa. Oda will have none of them. He will never trust a Takeda Bushi."

"And what about us?" I had never been in a city when it was conquered.

With a little stick he was holding Priest Jogen drew a figure in the dust at his feet. "Oda Nobunaga has little use for priests. He has fought them many times. In the battle of Hiei-zan he chopped heads off so many priests that their blood flowed like a river. I do not think he would trust me."

"Why did he kill the priests?" I was surprised. I thought priests were sacred.

"Oh, he had good reason to. The priests in that temple had grown rich. They kept an army of their own and thought the road to Buddha and the road of the sword were the same. They sided with one of Oda's enemies. They say that more than two thousand priests were killed."

"Then it is true that the blood must have run like a river. Is their temple very great and beautiful?"

"Temples, Saru, and were, for Oda burned them all down.

Not a building was left standing. He is a cruel man, but the priests were cruel, too. They fought other priests and burned a temple in Nara. They were sure they knew the great highway to Buddha and would not allow anyone else to follow their own little paths."

"I am glad that I am only a monkey," I said. "Oda would not care about what happened to a monkey."

"Oda Nobunaga does not care what happens to anyone except himself. Maybe, Saru, it would be wise to leave Kofuchu before he arrives. He does not trust priests, especially if they are of the Jodo sect. If a monkey and a poor priest got in his way, he would kill them as if they were a couple of flies."

"Look!" I exclaimed in a low voice. The Samurai was standing outside the gate, looking up and down our alley to see if anyone had noticed him before he stepped inside.

"You are welcome!" Priest Jogen rose and bowed. The Samurai bowed and smiled at me. "Saru, we shall have some tea." The priest led the Samurai to his little hut which contained one large room and a small lean-to kitchen. Luckily there were still embers left, and I soon heated the water. From the kitchen I could hear the voice of the Samurai, but I could not make out what he said. As I entered and took the teacups from the little wooden box where they were kept, the Samurai glanced at me and said: "Saru, the lord who once gave you a silver coin is dead." He looked expectantly at me, waiting for my reaction to his words.

"He was very old," I said.

"He was going blind. He called for my master, his son, as he died." The Samurai sighed. "I never revenged his son, and now it is too late."

"I think that it does not help the dead if we revenge them. How can we know if they want it?"

"You must forgive Saru for speaking his mind. It is a habit, I think, of his tribe." Priest Jogen smiled. "You have brought the cups. Now bring the tea, you tailless monkey!"

"So you have been inside the castle again?" I was pouring the tea for the Samurai and the priest, so I nodded in reply. "You met a friend there?" I frowned as I thought of Shiro. Was he a friend?

"I met someone I once knew. He is older than I am. He is a man now and strong, too. He is a litter carrier. He carries Katsuyori's wife when she goes to the temples to pray."

"Where does she pray?" The Samurai looked at me solemnly.

"Everywhere. Shiro says that he has carried her to every temple in Kofuchu. But that may not be true, for he often lies."

"And you don't?" The Samurai made a grimace meant to pass as a smile.

I looked very seriously at him, acting as if what he said was not a jest. "If my life depended on it, I would lie as fast as the fleetest horse could run, but I never lie for the pleasure of lying. Shiro does."

"Yes, there are people like that. I think sometimes that they could not tell the truth if their lives depended on it. I knew a Bushi once who was very brave. He had been in many battles and always in the very vanguard. Yet when he told of his adventures he always had to triple the men he had killed. The result was that no one believed him."

"I think that for Shiro it is a habit. I do not think that the words 'lie' or 'truth' have such meaning for him. Maybe when he tells a lie it becomes the truth to him."

"I do not think that Saru has ever lied to me in all the years I have known him." Priest Jogen looked kindly at me.

"I am sure I must have." I blushed, feeling certain that I did not deserve his kind words. "Shiro told me about the old lady who was killed because her son had fled. He told me, too, that if you have silver, then you can get a hostage out. Is that true?"

"It might be possible, if you know who to pay and have silver enough. I have thought of it but have not dared to try for fear that it could make things worse. If someone told that I had attempted to buy him with my silver, then Katsuyori would have us both killed. He has no love for me, and everyone knows this. It would be a brave man who tried to help me." The Samurai drew a leather purse from his sleeve and, turning to the priest, said, "Katsuyori-sama has taken over Lord Akiyama's mansion. I am still allowed the room where I have slept these last months, but strangers have been given the house. Here is all the silver which I can call mine. Will you keep it for me? I am afraid that it is far from enough to buy my wife's freedom. If Katsuyori decides to kill us both, then keep it and say some prayers for our souls' sake."

"I will keep it for you, Murakami-sama." The priest took the purse and put it down beside him.

"I once told you my name: Murakami Harutomo. Leave the word 'sama' for those who take pleasure in being called a lord. I am now almost as miserable a being as I was when I was a small child and Takeda Shingen's soldiers killed my brothers and my parents."

I was looking at the purse and hardly heard what he had said. "Your purse may still weigh enough to free your wife," I exclaimed. "To buy Katsuyori you would need a mountain of gold and to buy the other lords the same of silver. But there are others for sale for much less. Those who have never held a silver coin in their palm will do much for it. Let the masters be and let us buy their servants."

"But can one trust a man who will betray his master?" Murakami-san looked down at the mat he was sitting on, as if he expected to find an answer to his question there.

"Saru, one cannot trust such a man's honor." The priest shook his head.

"I think if one cannot trust their honor, one might be able to trust their greed." I laughed. "Murakami-san and Priest Jogen are good men," I thought, "and they may not lose their way on the road to Buddha. But in the alleys and paths of this world they would soon get lost."

"Are you thinking of your friend who carries the litter?" Murakami-san looked earnestly at me.

"Shiro would do anything for some silver coins. Or almost anything. He is not a friend of mine, although I once thought he was." It hurt to admit this. "I needed friends then, for I was very lonely. He knows many of the soldiers and I am sure the serving women as well. The food they are fed is hardly worth eating. Many of them are hungry. When a man is hungry, he will sell his soul for a dish of soba."

"But can one trust them?" Priest Jogen looked at me.

"If one cannot trust Takeda Katsuyori, then maybe one

has to run the risk of trusting others." Murakami-san looked at me intently.

"I do not know. I would not trust Shiro's honor as I am not sure he has any. But he is clever and, as I have said, he would do much for money. He is also very brave."

"Brave?" Murakami-san could not think anyone brave who was not honorable.

"Yes, brave. Some of the Ronins that turn robbers can be brave, too. They forget their honor. I don't think that Shiro ever had any. But he is still brave and very clever."

"You must not tell my name to him. That would be too dangerous if he should decide to betray us. But try and find out if he can, and is willing, to help us. As for the price, we could cover that palm of his in silver."

"I will search him out. I will be careful, and I will not offer him too much. I do not want his greed to grow too quickly. Whatever he is offered he will want more. It is best to start so low that one can double it. Besides, you will need money yourself."

"I could sell my . . . my swords." Murakami-san looked at the weapons in his obi. "Saru, you have given me hope. If you can find a way to free my wife, I shall call you Saru-sama."

Priest Jogen laughed. "Lord Monkey. The ruler of all the monkeys in the world. Truly, Saru, if you can do it, I will bow to you and call you Saru-sama, too!"

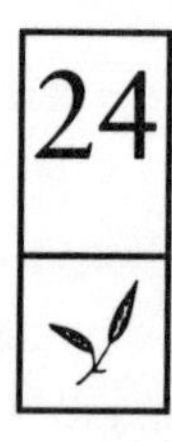

24 *My Plan for Rescuing Murakami-san's Wife*

I was so eager to search for Shiro that I left the temple at the same time as Murakami-san. As we came near the entrance gate he turned to me and said: "It is best we are not seen together." I bowed and stepped aside to let him go through, but he paused. "I was once a boy like you. I, too, had to be a man when by age I still should have sat on my mother's lap. I was given no choice but to grow up. I, too, was lonely then. Once I had a friend, but he got killed." Murakami-san put his hand on my shoulder and pressed it. Then he turned abruptly and left. I waited a little to give him time to reach the road that led to Tsutsujigasaki Castle.

I did not want to go too near the castle. I was afraid that some of the soldiers would recognize me if I was seen there too often. Instead I went to alleys and paths near the castle. Here were several little taverns, places where soldiers drank and ate when they could afford it. I saw no sign of Shiro, but I hardly expected to be so lucky. I was just about to give up when I met not Shiro, but Nami, carrying a heavy basket. She greeted me and put down her basket for a moment, glad to have found an excuse to rest. "I am on an errand for my father," she said and smiled.

"Shall I carry it for you?" I asked. I wanted to find out if she knew Shiro.

"Why should you? Men don't carry things for women," Nami grumbled.

"But you are not a woman, and I am not a man. The basket seems to be heavy."

"It is, and I have carried it from afar. My father does not lift a finger if he can help it." Suddenly she laughed. "That is true, you are only a monkey, and maybe monkeys carry things."

I lifted the heavy basket. "Monkeys swing from branch to branch in the trees. They never carry anything. Come, and I will walk you to the castle. Is your father a good cook? Does he stir the porridge he cooks for the soldiers?"

"He cooks better things for them if they can pay. There are chickens and rice in there." Nami nodded at the basket I was carrying.

"Sake as well?" I asked, and Nami nodded. Her father must keep a little tavern of his own inside the castle, I thought. I felt certain it was not permitted. Much went on inside Takeda Katsuyori's castle that the master did not know about.

"They say that Katsuyori-sama is going to move everyone to the new Shimpu Castle. It is on top of a mountain." Nami nodded her head as she spoke.

"Will everyone be going there?" I asked, setting down the heavy basket. Besides, I did not want to get to the castle too soon.

"My father says he is not going. I think we shall leave. I have an aunt in Sagami. Perhaps we will go there." Nami paused for a moment. "It is out in the country, I shall miss Kofuchu. There I shall be put to work in the fields."

"They will make you tend the pigs," I said and grinned.

"Maybe I will get married. One of the soldiers has asked me," Nami said. "But he is pretty old."

"Maybe he has pigs, too, or a mother who will beat you." I realized that she was still a child and felt sure that the soldier had only been making fun of her.

"Why don't you marry me?" Nami asked. "We could live in a tree!"

"But what if you fell down? Are you used to climbing trees?"

"There is a big tree near my father's cookhouse. I can climb that." Nami's face grew serious as she pointed to a man coming down the street. "That is the soldier who asked me to marry him."

There are people one takes an instant dislike to, and this soldier was one of them. He swaggered along, looking at everyone and the world with contempt. "Who does he belong to? What Samurai is his master?"

"I am not sure. He is a bowman. He may be one of Katsuyori's. He often guards the women's house. He comes to my father's hut to drink."

"I think he is too old for you." The soldier had spied us and was crossing the street.

"What have you got in the basket?" he asked, pinching Nami's cheek. "Something good?" He looked down into it. "Chickens!" he exclaimed and then laughingly declared, "I think I will take one."

"They are my father's!" Nami screamed and grabbed the

basket. The soldier acted as if he was going to take it from her, and Nami swung it behind her, ready to defend it.

"I think I like it cooked. Tell your father to keep half of one for me." With a fleeting glance at me, the soldier passed on as if he owned Kofuchu.

"I would be careful if I married him. He needs no mother to beat you—he would do it himself."

"I wouldn't marry him anyway." Nami tossed her head. "He is nothing but a soldier. My father says that they will all be killed when Oda Nobunaga comes."

I nodded. I saw that the soldier had gone into one of the small taverns. "I would keep away from him if I were you."

"My father likes him. He often has money, not copper mons but silver. I'd better get back." She stepped away so that I could take the basket once more.

I shouldered it, and we walked on.

"Do you know the men who carry the litter when Katsuyori's wife goes to pray?" I asked, making the question sound of no importance.

"One is young. They sometimes come to my father's place. I like the young one. He once gave me a copper mon."

"Yes, that would be Shiro," I thought. "He would give a mon even to a child." We were now near the entrance to the castle, and I gave the basket back to Nami. "If I am to marry you," I said and grinned, "then we must meet again."

"Tomorrow?" Nami's expression was solemn.

"When the sun is highest in the sky, the same place as I met you today." I felt bad, for she had thought the soldier had meant it when he said he would marry her and now I am sure she believed I would.

"I will come," she whispered and then ran toward the gate, the basket swinging beside her. I watched as she entered and saw that the soldiers merely shouted something at her. She was a sweet little girl and all the soldiers were fond of her, as they would be of a favorite puppy.

I did not find Shiro that day, but I felt my meeting with Nami had been fortunate. I had learned more of what was going on inside the castle. It seemed to me that more of the soldiers thought of fleeing than of staying to fight the invading army of Oda Nobunaga. That evening I told Priest Jogen what I had learned and of my plan. If I could pay enough, it would not be too difficult to bribe Shiro and his partner to carry Murakami-san's wife out of the castle. The difficulty would be in getting her out of the house where the hostages were kept. I thought the soldier I had met in the street too much of a scoundrel to trust. He would think it the right thing to do, to take your money and then betray you.

"Are you not afraid?" Priest Jogen looked searchingly at me.

I thought for a moment before answering. "No, but I know I should be. Maybe later I will be afraid. Now I am just thinking of the plan and of everything that can go wrong."

"Saru, you have seen the place where the executions take place, the sightless eyes of the heads and the bodies of those that have been crucified? That will be your fate."

I nodded. It was true—if caught. But somehow I could not believe it would happen. "Are you frightened?" I asked.

"No man can call himself brave before he has stared death

in the face. I think of myself as a coward. It is easier than to imagine oneself a hero who does not know fear."

"Yet there are many who think themselves brave without having stood that test," I argued.

"Oh, they are fools," Priest Jogen said contemptuously. "You know bragging is not the greatest fault a man can have, yet I dislike a braggart above almost all others. Maybe that is not to my credit, for my dislike may stem from envy. Maybe I, too, want to brag about myself but dare not do it. Most people fail in what they want to do. The lucky ones are spared knowing it."

"I do not know what I want to do." I frowned as I tried to think about it.

"You will find the road to Buddha." Priest Jogen laughed. "Without ever searching for the way, you will find it."

"You are always talking about the road as if it were a street like the one that leads through Kofuchu to Tsutsujigasaki Castle. Maybe there is no road, no path. Maybe it is more like climbing a mountain. You go ever upward, through the forest, up and down ravines until at last you reach the summit."

"And what if it is the wrong mountain you have climbed? What if there is no Buddha there? What if it is Yamamba who sits there?"

I laughed when I understood that my mountain was no different from the roads or the way that Priest Jogen had talked about. "If Yamamba is sitting there, then I shall be made into monkey stew."

"It is a strange story, good for scaring children when they

do not behave. Yamamba, the old woman who eats people. Are you scared of her?"

I shook my head. "I never believed in her, even when I was tiny. Aya-san used to frighten me with her. But you see, I have always lived in Kofuchu. Now if I had lived on the mountain in a lonely hut, then maybe she would have scared me. Do you think there is such a thing as ghosts?"

"I am sure there are, Saru, but I do not think they can harm us. I have listened to many stories about ghosts. But I have never met one myself."

I shrugged my shoulders. I had lived too long alone in the darkness of the night to be scared of them. "I don't think there are such things as ghosts," I said, and looked at the priest.

"Most people believe in them, and in goblins, ogres, and dragons that live in our lakes. I like some of those tales. I have never seen a dragon, but when I look at the still waters of a lake I like to think that a dragon lives in the depths below. There must be something that cannot be explained," Priest Jogen concluded. "Something which scares us a little because we do not understand it."

"Oh, there is enough to scare me without Yamamba or ghosts. The soldier I saw today scared me. Those who can kill with the same ease with which we squash a fly. I do not understand them. It is as if something is missing within them." I rose, for it was time to sleep.

"What will you do tomorrow, Saru? Remember, do not mention Murakami or his wife's name. Not before you have gotten his permission."

I opened the door. It was a beautiful night. The sky was

filled with stars, and a sliver of a crescent moon hung among them. "I know I shall try and get a message to Shiro. I shall meet Nami again. But I do not know how much time we have. We must choose a time when Takeda Katsuyori has gone to his new castle but before the hostages have been moved." I bowed to the priest and closed the door behind me. "Tomorrow," I thought. "The days fly by and I do not know how many days we have, how many tomorrows are spared us."

25 *A Proposal of Marriage*

I wonder if I could do now what I did then. No, I would be filled with fears of failure, doubts that would have made decisions difficult. As I walked to my appointment with Nami, I felt so certain that my plan would succeed that I lightheadedly skipped along. I had a few copper mons in my sleeve. I thought I would give one to Nami and keep the others to treat Shiro with. Nami was waiting for me, and the smile on her face hurt me.

"I can't stay long," Nami said, bowing to me. "My father wants me back."

"Did the soldier come and eat his chicken?" I asked.

"Oh, he drank and ate until very late. The cocks had almost crowed before he and his friends left. They drank so much sake that my father had no more to serve them, and they made so much noise that my father was afraid some of the masters would hear them. But Katsuyori-sama is away and has taken most of the Samurais with him."

"How long will he be away? Do you know?" I asked excitedly.

"I don't know. He has gone to get help, so the soldiers say. They said he has gone to see Hojo Ujimasa. But they also said he would get no help there. They said his fate is sealed and the end of the Takedas has come."

"Are they staying to fight?"

"Not the old man, the one who wanted to marry me. He said that when Takeda Katsuyori-sama did not come to the aid of those who fought for him in Takatenjin Castle but left them to be slaughtered by Tokugawa Iyeyasu, all men lost faith in him. He was not going to die for someone unworthy to lay down one's life for. But he was very drunk then." Nami laughed. "I saw him fall, just outside my father's hut. He cursed and lay still for ever so long before he finally got up. But why do you want to know about all this?"

I did not answer her question but asked another instead. "When is your father going to Sagami?"

"My father is greedy. He will stay as long as he makes money. My mother says we should leave now, but he will not listen to her. He just tells her to keep quiet or he will beat her."

"Does he do that often?" I asked, thinking that there were advantages in being an orphan, for I felt sure that if her mother got beaten, then poor Nami had not escaped the same treatment.

"Only when he is drunk. Then I hide and don't come home before he is asleep." Nami frowned, adding, "But it is not so often now, for he dares not drink too much for fear that someone should leave without paying."

I could not help laughing, but, seeing Nami's frown

deepen, I stopped. "It must be hard for you," I said.

"That is why I am thinking of getting married. Would you beat me? Would you beat me if I hadn't done anything, like my father sometimes does?"

"I don't think I would beat you at all." It was hard for me to keep a serious expression.

"My mother says that all men say that before they marry you. But that you can't trust any of them."

I smiled. "That may be true, but then would it not be better not to marry?"

"Oh, no, that would be shameful. Where would I live? I would rather have a husband who beat me than be beaten by my father." Nami shook her head as she contemplated the two possibilities, neither of which seemed very pleasant.

"Tell me, Nami, how old are you?" I asked.

"I was born in the first year of Genki, so my mother says."

"Then you are only ten years old, Nami. That is too young to marry. We must wait a few years."

Nami nodded unhappily. I had heard that the great lords sometimes married when they were very young but decided not to tell Nami that. "You will have to wait for me at least two years."

"Will you come for me then?" Nami looked eagerly at me, waiting for my reply.

"I will," I said, and at that moment I believed my words. "Here." I took the copper mon out of my sleeve and gave it to her.

"I shall keep it." Nami held it in her hand and looked at it. Her sleeves were short, and she tucked it into her obi instead. "Now, I must go. When will you be here again?"

"When you can get away. But there is something I want you to do for me."

"Yes. What is it you want me to do? I am not scared of doing almost anything."

"I want you to find the youngest of the two litter carriers. His name used to be Shiro, but he may use another one now. Tell him that I want to see him. Tell me to meet me in that place where I bought him soba."

"Will you buy me soba, too? I like noodles."

"Some day soon, I shall buy you a big portion of soba."

"Good." Nami nodded in satisfaction. "I must go now because my father will get angry if I stay away too long. I will find your friend for you and tell him what you said." Nami started to walk back to the castle when she suddenly realized that I was her future husband. She turned around and bowed very low to me. I returned her bow, remembering not to bow as low as she had done, for a husband should never do that.

As I walked back to the temple I thought of Nami. There were many children like her. They were no more wanted, or as much wanted, as the work they could perform. Cats take care of their kittens for at least as long as they cannot take care of themselves. But that was not always true of human beings. I had been told that sometimes newborn girls, if there were too many girls in the family, would be set out in the mountains to die and be eaten by wild animals. But would not parents who did that be reborn as cockroaches? Perhaps the girl they had set out to die would be reborn in the family of a great lord.

When I got back to the temple there were people who had come to pray. I could see several pairs of straw sandals in front of the steps. I could hear Priest Jogen praying inside. I hoped they had brought us something good to eat. But the sandals were old and well worn, so I did not expect much. "Saru," a voice so low that it was not much more than a whisper called me. I looked around but could see no one. Then I noticed that the door to the priest's hut was ajar. Someone was there, and I guessed it was Murakami-san. I walked across our little courtyard. When I came to the door I stood still for a moment and listened. "Come in, and close the door behind you!" the same voice commanded.

The Samurai was sitting cross-legged on the mat. As I entered he gestured to me to sit down. For a while we sat facing each other in silence. I waited for him to speak as it would be impolite for me to speak first. Finally he said, "Saru, I fear we have waited too long." I knew what he meant but said nothing, only bending my head a little to show that I had understood. "A friend—and I have few—told me to flee."

"And will you?" I asked.

"How can I, Saru? Where would I go? The spirit of my wife whom I left to be killed would follow me. I would forever see her eyes looking sadly at me, telling me of betrayal. No, I shall wait here and maybe bargain my life for hers."

"Katsuyori has gone and so have most of the Samurais. They say he has gone to seek aid from Hojo Ujimasa. Now is the time we must flee."

"How?" Murakami-san looked at me in despair. "No one would dare to help us. Everyone knows that my life is over. Takeda Katsuyori has sworn, so my friend told me, that when he returns he shall put to death all those who are not loyal to him. When someone asked him who they were, he mentioned my name first of all."

"There are those who can be bought. You would not know them, they are too lowly born for you to notice. They fear that when the Takedas fall, their lives may end as well. They have no wish to commit seppuko, no wish to slash their bellies, only to fill them. How much silver may I promise them?"

"All I have. Priest Jogen keeps it for me. I shall tell him that you can take what you want."

"I thought we had more time, but maybe it is best like this. I must go to seek a friend." I rose and was about to bow before I left when it suddenly occurred to me that I had to ask permission to tell who it was among the hostages we wanted freed. "Can I, with care, use your name now?"

"Yes, it does not matter now. Did I tell you that my wife's name is Aki-hime?" Murakami spoke the name as if it were sacred.

"I shall do my very best," I said and bowed. The Samurai rose and bowed as deeply as I had. As I crossed the courtyard I mumbled the name to myself. "Hime" is an honorable title only given to the daughters of the great lords who rule our countries and our lives.

Haru-san greeted me in her soba shop as a favorite customer. Remembering how kind she had been to me when I was a little beggar child, it pleased me now to be treated this way. I almost expected Shiro to be there, but the hut was empty. I sat down on the mat in front of her one little table and ordered soba.

"Saru," she said, her round face serious now. "Some soldier said that when Oda Nobunaga's army comes they will burn all of Kofuchu. Why should they do that? Do not his soldiers eat soba and drink sake?"

"They come from Owari, and there they eat cats and mice, which they fry on sticks when they have burned down a town. Nobunaga himself lives off his enemies. How they are cooked I don't know. But they do drink sake I have been told." I tried to look as serious as I could. For a moment Haru-san thought that I meant what I had said, then she burst out laughing.

"All the cats in Kofuchu are skinny, not worth roasting. But, Saru, I hear that they are hard on their enemies."

"Haru-san, Oda Nobunaga is no fool. What good will it do him to burn down the town? Where would his soldiers sleep? Where would they eat? It is true that he is cruel. Too many have told me that for me not to believe it." I looked at Haru-san. "How many like her die or have their houses burned down when war comes?" I wondered.

"The water is boiling, I will come with your soba. Today is now, and tomorrow must take care of itself."

I ate my soba slowly, deciding how much I could tell Haru-san. I trusted her, but she liked to gossip too much. She gossiped about her neighbors, and a tale told to her was twice as long when she retold it.

"Haru-san, remember the young man who came with me when I was here last?" I asked.

"He was a handsome youngster! When I saw him I wished I was a young girl again." Haru-san laughed.

"If he comes looking for me, could you send someone to the temple to tell me? I shall come right away. Serve him some soba, and give him a small pitcher of sake as well. He may come today, but if not, he is sure to come tomorrow." Haru-san looked at me as if she expected me to say more. "He is an old friend," I finally said.

"Surely I will, Saru, I will send Kura." She was a girl who lived with Haru-san. Some people said she was her daughter. She was lame, but that did not keep her from running nearly as fast as anyone else. She frightened me a little, for she would sometimes say the strangest things.

When I left, Kura was sitting on the steps leading up to the hut. I nodded to her. She held up a finger, pointing it toward the sky. "Saru-san, I saw an eagle today. It flew around and around above the castle." As she spoke, she made great circles in the air with her finger. "When the eagle comes, little birds best take care." She laughed a wild cackling laughter and, pointing at me, said, "Saru, you are a little bird."

"I am a monkey, Kura, and eagles don't eat monkeys. But still I shall be careful." I hurried away, but her laughter, or the memory of it, stayed with me until I was back in the temple.

26 *The Power of Silver Coins*

I did not dare go away from the temple, for I felt certain that as soon as Shiro had got my message he would come. Our meeting place, the soba shop, and its memories of noodles and sake would make him hurry. The sun had just set when Kura came to fetch me. She giggled as she told me that my friend had come. "He is very handsome," she said and combed her short hair with her fingers.

I wondered how old Kura was. She looked ageless, but she could not be much more than thirty years old. "I will come right away. Tell him to wait," I said as I put away the broom I had been sweeping the temple with.

"Saru-san, will anyone ever marry me?" Kura asked, looking at me earnestly.

"Ask Haru-san to find a husband for you," I suggested. I had had enough of women who wanted to marry.

"She won't. She said that no one would want to marry me." Suddenly Kura laughed as if what she had said was amusing. "When she dies and I get the soba shop, then I will find a man who will marry me."

"She is waiting for that. She is more like a child than a

grownup," I thought as I told her impatiently to hurry home. I wanted to talk to Priest Jogen before I left. I watched her running across the courtyard, her left leg dragging.

"Murakami-san has told me I can have what money I need of his. Now I just want one silver ryo."

Priest Jogen sighed. He was sitting on the mat in his room reading. "Here is one. It is mine." The priest took the silver coin from inside the sleeve of his kimono. "What do you want it for?"

"I have to have it so I can show it. The sight of silver to a poor man is like the smell of a roasted chicken to someone who is starving."

"You know that if you manage to get Murakami's wife out of the castle we must flee. Katsuyori will send soldiers after us, and if they catch us, then we will never see the sun rise again."

I tucked away the silver and laughed. "They shan't catch us. We shall go to that temple by the sea where you know the priest. You said he is a good man."

"I borrowed some robes from a priest who thinks kindly of me. We shall travel like monks going on a pilgrimage."

"That is good," I said. I was pleased that Priest Jogen thought enough of my plan to enter into it. "I shall be back soon to tell you when we shall need those robes."

I ran all the way to Haru-san's shop. Shiro was greedily eating his second portion of soba when I arrived. I noticed that the sake pitcher was empty and ordered another one. Haru-san brought it and a cup for me as well. I poured sake for both of us, then lifted my cup. "I have something important to tell you," I said as I put it down. I looked at Haru-san and made a motion toward the kitchen with my head. She understood and left us alone. Luckily few of the soldiers in Kofuchu had money to waste on soba and sake, and we were alone.

"I expected as much. Food and drink do not come free in this town," Shiro said. I noticed that he had emptied his sake cup when we toasted each other and I had taken only a sip.

"You said to me when we met last that you wanted to leave Kofuchu. A beggar on the road usually has an empty stomach, and there are few people who will care to fill it. With money in one's purse one travels better."

"That is true. Innkeepers are born misers." Shiro grinned. "My ears are open even to a monkey's tale."

I leaned toward him and told him what I wanted done, speaking softly so that Haru-san could not hear me. It took some time to tell. Shiro looked intently at me, following each word as I spoke.

"There is much danger in this plan of yours. I see my head on a spike, and I do not like that sight. Who is the woman?"

I poured the last drop of sake into his cup. "She is the wife of the Samurai Murakami. Her name is Aki-hime."

"Neither sake nor soba will free a hostage. Nor will copper coins." Shiro shook his head.

I drew the silver ryo from my sleeve and held it in my open palm. "This coin has many brothers," I said as I returned it to its place.

"It is a family much liked, I am sure. But I tell you it needs to be large."

"Soon Oda Nobunaga's army will be here, and then the lucky ones will be beggars."

Shiro glanced at my sleeve. "That is true. The unlucky ones will be where silver won't help them," he said. "If you have as many silver coins as there are months in a year and maybe a few more, it could be done."

"I told you, my coin has many brothers. They are all alike and equally heavy." As a fisherman knows when he has caught a fish on his line, I knew that Shiro would be willing to try.

"You are right. Both I and the other beast of burden on that litter have long been tired of our work. True, too, I do not think the soldier will stop us at the gate. There is a guard at the hostage house who would also like his purse well filled. I must think how it could be done." Shiro winked at me. "Maybe it would help my courage to have just one more of those very small pitchers of sake."

I called Haru-san and ordered more sake. She knelt by us as she poured it.

"Your soba was very good. When I become ruler of Kai I shall have you as my cook," Shiro told her.

"Oh, I should like that. Are you moving into the castle as soon as Katsuyori moves out?"

"Oh, he is my brother. I am here in disguise." Shiro emptied his cup, and Haru-san filled it up again. "Saru here is no monkey. He is Oda Nobunaga himself, who has come to spy out the land."

"Pay no attention to him, Haru-san, he is just a Tanuki who has taken human shape, and you know what they are like, eating and drinking is all they care about. Drink up, Tanuki, I want to go home," I said in annoyance.

Shiro laughed, and for a moment I thought he might demand more sake. Then he rose, bowed to Haru-san, and we left. It was now dark outside, but the moon had just risen over the mountains.

"Give me the silver coin," Shiro demanded.

When I did not hand it over, he asked if I did not trust him.

"Maybe not. But then I have to, don't I?" I took the coin from my sleeve, which was now empty as I had spent the copper mons. Shiro took the coin and looked at it carefully. It shone briefly in the light from the moon. Then he spat on it and tucked it away.

"You had to use that as bait in order to catch me. Now it is my turn to use it. Any fool can promise silver, but what is such a promise worth? The sight of the coin will help convince them that there is more to be gained."

"That's true, but do not tell the name of the woman before you are sure that the guard is willing to help. There might be silver to be earned in betraying us as well."

Shiro shook his head. "Katsuyori does not part with his silver. They say he has got a sack full of his father's gold as well. But I do not believe that. If you can promise maybe twenty pieces of silver it can be done. But it must be done soon, tomorrow or the day after. When Katsuyori comes home it will be more difficult. While the cat is away, the mice grow bold."

Shiro was right, he needed that little piece of silver. I had no idea how many pieces of silver the Samurai's purse contained but promised enough to pay whatever was needed.

"I liked the soba." Shiro laughed. "When the sun is well over the mountain tomorrow I shall meet you here. Then I shall tell you how much more of your treasure I shall need." He turned and walked toward the castle. I returned to the temple, eager to find out if we had indeed the money which I had promised.

Priest Jogen had buried the Samurai's purse in the corner of his hut. On top of the place where he had hidden it, he had placed an iron pot with some flowers. I thought it silly. Would not a thief suspect and search that place first of all?

"Now Saru, remember that this is not ours. It was given us in trust." The priest weighed the leather bag in his hand. "If they are not all copper coins there must be at least twenty silver ones in it," I thought. I grew impatient as Priest Jogen fumbled with the string fastening. Finally he emptied the money on the tiny table. The coins made a big pile. There were some copper mons among the silver, but I could see that there was enough. We stacked them in piles of five to count them. When we had finished there were seven piles plus a handful of copper coins. For a while we sat in silence, looking at our treasure. Neither of us had ever seen such riches before. Finally the priest put the coins back in the purse. I took five mons and put them in my sleeve, for I would need those tomorrow to pay for Shiro's noodles.

"Saru, bring the young man here tomorrow. We must plan where to meet and how to hide the litter at least for a few hours. They must not find it right away. Every hour that we gain will be more precious than even silver or gold."

"I have thought of it. They may find out in any case that

the litter has been brought here, but it would be best if it left again. I know of a ruin not far from here. The roof is gone, but the walls are still standing. There it would be hidden from sight."

Priest Jogen nodded. Looking around his little hut, he sighed. "I shall miss my hut, maybe more than the temple. The place is filled with dreams that I have dreamed while living here. You know, it is the first place that has ever been truly mine. When I was a novice, there were so many of us sleeping in the hut that it felt as if you could not call the air you breathed your own."

"If there is no hut in that temple by the sea we shall build one. I wonder what the sea is like? I cannot imagine it!"

"It has a hundred voices, Saru. Sometimes it shouts in anger, and at other times it whispers to you. It clothes itself differently each day, when the wind whips it, then it wears a cape of white foam." Priest Jogen smiled, recalling it. "Oh, I should like to see it once more."

"We shall soon be there," I said and felt certain of it.

27 *Shiro Meets Priest Jogen*

I slept badly that night. In my dreams I saw Shiro and his friend come trotting with the litter and when we opened it there was no one inside. It was as if all the doubts and fears I should have had in the daytime at night came to give me troubled sleep. I woke as the sun rose and went to boil some rice for our breakfast. I could hear that Priest Jogen was awake as well. The rice was just ready when he came into our little kitchen.

"I slept badly thinking that this might be one of my last nights in my own home. Do you know, Saru, if Murakami-san's wife is small or tall?"

"I think she is not tall," I said, remembering that Nami had said she was tiny.

"I got two novice gowns, one for you and one for her, but I was worried that it would not fit her."

"Will Murakami-san cut his hair?" I asked, for he kept his hair in the elaborate style of a Samurai, and a Buddhist monk or priest has his head shaven.

"I have two straw hats with wide brims which will hide their faces. But can she walk fast and far? She cannot be used to it. It will not matter as soon as we are out of Kai, where Takeda Katsuyori rules; then we can take our time and fit our day's march to hers. But the first few days we must make haste."

"When she cannot walk any farther we must carry her." I felt there was no reason to worry about that so long as she was still in the castle.

When the sun had risen above the mountains, I set out. As I came near Haru-san's soba shop it occurred to me that if Shiro had betrayed us soldiers would be waiting to catch me when I came along. The only living thing near her little hut was a mangy dog. It came up wagging its tail but at the same time expecting me to kick it. "Our world," I thought, "can be divided into two, those who kick and those who are kicked." I scratched the dog's ears, and it looked up at me with docile eyes. I had nothing to give it but decided to ask Haru-san for some scraps if she had any.

I opened the door cautiously, ready to flee if soldiers were hidden inside. Only Haru-san's round and pleasant face greeted me.

"Is your friend coming? If so, I'd better heat the water." Haru-san smiled.

"I shall wait for him, but if you have some tea it would be welcome." I sat down by her little table. "Where is your girl, Kura?" I asked, though I did not care at all where she was.

"I have sent her on an errand. Did you need her?"

"No, I just wondered. She is worried that she will never be married, or so she told me."

"So she tells everyone." Haru-san laughed. "But she falls in love each day, poor thing, and always with the most handsome of men. Once she fell in love with a Samurai. Every time he left the castle she would follow him like a dog or a shadow."

"What happened then?"

"He hit her, and pretty hard. She came home crying, and since then she has had no love for Samurais." Haru-san brought me tea. "I know people think that she is mine. She is not. I found her naked and starving and took her in. There is no harm in her."

"There is a dog outside. Do you not have a scrap of something I can give it?"

Haru-san shook her head. "If you feed it, it will follow you. It is better not." But then she went to the kitchen and came out with what looked like a hen's head and, opening the door, threw it to the cur.

"Now it will follow you," I said and smiled.

Haru-san shrugged and glanced at me. "Oh, I take care of all sorts of strays," she said pointedly.

"And do they not wag their tails in gratitude?" I asked.

"Some do, but some will bite your hand." Haru-san closed the door. "I'd better prepare some soba for your friend. He is the kind of customer I like, with a good appetite and thirst."

"There are lots of people in Kofuchu with empty bellies and thirsty throats."

"Yes, Saru-san, but they also have empty purses and no rich friends who are willing to pay for them." Haru-san took my teapot to refill it.

Shiro looked very pleased with himself as he entered. I was sure that he was the bearer of good news. He sat down opposite me. Haru-san brought him a cup and knelt down beside him as she poured his tea. "Have you had so good a breakfast that you cannot eat a little of my noodles?" she asked in a girlish tone of voice.

"I have had no breakfast that even a hungry dog would brag of. We are all half starved in the castle, at least those among us who are beasts of burden and not proper men."

"I shall make it a double portion." Haru-san glanced at me for my permission. When I nodded she rushed into her kitchen and closed the sliding door behind her.

"What news?" I asked in so low a voice that I doubt if it could be heard in the kitchen.

"I am as hungry as a mother fox with cubs," Shiro said loudly, then more softly, "tomorrow, about this time."

I rose swiftly and slid open the door. Haru-san was busy cooking. "Make me a portion as well."

"Best not to talk here," I whispered.

"They are expecting Katsuyori-sama home soon. They say we shall be moving to his new castle then." Shiro kept gossiping about his master, as all servants do, until the soba came. Then with great gusto he began to eat, making as much noise as five men as he sucked the noodles into his mouth.

As I paid Haru-san I wondered if she had understood or suspected that our meetings had not been merely for her soba and sake. She took my coppers and bowed low to both of us as we left.

Once outside Shiro told me that he had managed to bribe the guard at the women's house and that he and his partner would bring the litter through the gate at the hour of the snake. "The guards there will not dare to challenge us. They would not risk finding Takeda Katsuyori's wife inside. It would be more than their heads are worth."

"Can you trust the guard at the women's house? He might take the money and then raise the alarm." I felt certain that the soldier he was talking about was the one who had promised to marry Nami.

"There is no man more untrustworthy in Tsutsujigasaki than him." Shiro laughed. "He is as thorough a scoundrel as it should ever be your misfortune to meet. I have no doubt that he will turn robber and that his head will end up on a stake."

"And such a man we have to trust," I said.

"He is brave and greedy enough to dare anything. He and one of the cooks have been selling our lord's rice. He knows that I know and that if he tells tales, I have some to tell as well. Do not worry. He is safe enough because he is dishonest. But once we have left he may decide to sell the news to one of the more foolish Samurais. When we have delivered what we have promised, I suggest you run quicker than rabbits."

"How much has he asked for?"

"First he claimed he would not dare do it unless he was paid in gold. I laughed at that, and then he suggested ten silver coins. I said that that would do for Katsuyori's wife, but I had no interest in her. I showed him my coin and said that he would receive five of those. He eyed it greedily, and we settled on six. I gave him the coin I had. Can you give me five more?"

We were by the entrance gate to our temple. I stopped for

a moment to tell Shiro that the priest would like to see him. As for the money, we had enough to pay the six coins to the soldier and as much each to Shiro and his partner.

"Priests are of two kinds, honest, wearing out their straw sandals on the road to Buddha, or worse scoundrels than the bandits who hide in mountains and rob poor travelers of what little they have. Lead me to him, and I shall tell you which kind you have fallen in with."

"The only person Priest Jogen would steal from would be himself. When I was a child he would often rob himself of his dinner to give it to me." I led Shiro to the priest's hut.

What always surprised me about Shiro was his ability to change as circumstances demanded. To Priest Jogen he was humble without being subservient. He spoke about his plan and what would happen tomorrow without ever bragging of how clever he had been. Again he warned that we would have to flee as fast as we could, for the guard could not be trusted.

"If he should ask where we are fleeing to, tell him that you are not sure but you heard us mention Tokugawa Iyeyasu." Priest Jogen smiled cunningly. "Be vague, for too strong a scent will make him suspicious."

Shiro smiled and nodded.

Priest Jogen gave Shiro the five coins, knotting them into a piece of cloth. "Do not give them to him before you leave. Only at the last moment should he have them," he admonished.

"Do not worry. He shall keep his promise, even though it may be for the first time in his life." Shiro rose and bowed deeply to the priest. I followed him outside as far as our gate.

"Well, what kind of priest is he?" I asked.

"I think he is well on his way to becoming a Buddha." Shiro grinned. "I have no such vocation. I shall follow the road of the sword. It is straighter and more comfortable to walk on." Shiro's face grew serious. "Yours is a better road, I know, but it is not for me. Till tomorrow." Shiro waved and walked down the little alley. When he reached the larger road a shadow ran out from a bush. It was Kura. She had fallen in love again, this time with Shiro.

28 *I Have My Head Shaven*

At sunset Murakami-san came to ask for news. When we told him that the very next day—if all went well—he should be reunited with his wife, he looked pained, as if this news was not to his liking. Seeing the surprise on our faces, he explained why.

"Many moons have passed since I last saw my wife. I had given up all hope and you have lit that hope again." Murakami-san smiled and glanced at me. "But now I cannot believe that it will happen. Fate has been kind to me at times. Twice since we married my wife has had to face death. The first time my servant saved her. Now if she is to be saved a second time, she will owe her life to a boy. I want it to happen, yet I cannot believe it. You say tomorrow at the hour of the snake. The hours until then will stretch like years."

"I think you will see your wife again. No, I feel sure of it." Priest Jogen put his hand on the Samurai's shoulder. "Do not worry. She will be saved."

"If not, then I shall follow her wherever she has gone." Murakami-san looked down at the ground and suddenly laughed. "How ungrateful I have been! I should be busy thanking you, and instead I behave as if you had brought me bad news. I am sorry." Murakami-san bowed to each of us.

In Priest Jogen's hut Murakami-san put on the priest's robe. Although it fit him, there was no doubt in my mind that he still looked like a Samurai. Priest Jogen took the big straw hat and put it on his head. It hid his hair and shaded his face. The swords were still visible under the robe. "I will get rid of the swords as soon as we are safe." Murakami-san took off the robe. "Until we are out of Takeda territory they may be of use." He smiled. "To gain these swords I once would have ventured my soul and now . . . now they do not matter anymore, they are but two pieces of iron. I will not sell them, I shall dig a hole and bury them—a grave for what I once was."

"I think it is best that you carry them over your shoulder. I shall find something to wrap them in." Priest Jogen eyed the weapons. "We must make it look like a bundle of no importance. Tell me, how tall is your wife? The same as Saru?"

The Samurai looked at me, his head tilted to one side as he judged my height. "No bigger," he said, "but much more beautiful."

"Till tomorrow. I shall come early and wait here, for I shall not sleep much tonight." Murakami-san looked at us both and said, "With two friends like you, even a poor man would be rich." Just as he was about to open the door, he took something from his sleeve and turned to the priest. "I think it best you keep our money. If I should die, will you protect my wife?"

"You will not die. You will have a long journey left. But if something should happen, I shall protect your wife as if she were my sister."

Murakami-san opened his fist. On his palm lay a large gold coin. The priest and I stared at it, neither of us having seen a gold coin before. "It is very old. It was given to me and now I give it to you." He slipped the coin into the priest's hand.

"I shall keep it with the other money." Priest Jogen put it in his sleeve and bowed.

"They are different from us," I said when the Samurai had left.

"Not really, Saru." Priest Jogen smiled and dropped the gold coin into the purse. "In a way, I think most people choose the road of the sword, even those with only a spade as their weapon. What is the difference between Takeda Katsuyori and that robber child you told me about? True, Katsuyori has a sama added to his name, the lord of Kai, but in truth he is a fool."

"Oh yes, but still they are different from us. The sword, their clothes. It makes a difference. Nezumi dreamed of being a Samurai, but he knew he wasn't."

"And you, Saru? What is your dream? Have you dreamed the same dream as the rat?"

I laughed. "But I am different, too, for I am a monkey—and one who listens but does not speak. When I was very small I used to dream that my father was not a humble soldier carrying a spear but a great officer in splendid clothes with swords in his obi. I soon realized that this was a fool's dream. I am what I am and that is enough."

"I think I shall have to change you a little, Saru." The priest grinned and looked at my hair. I knew what he meant and ran my hand through my hair. I did not like the idea of having my head shaven but knew that all young men who aspired to become monks or priests had their heads shaven. I shrugged and said, "It will grow again."

The priest owned a mirror, one of the few valuables he had. When I saw myself in it, I was surprised to see that my ears stuck out now that I had lost my hair. I grumbled a bit and put on the novice gown. "No one will recognize you now." The priest laughed. "A bald and tailless monkey."

"I shall carry my own clothes with me, and as soon as we are by the sea I shall put them on again." I could see that my words hurt the priest, for he looked at me solemnly. "Someday maybe I shall put this gown on again, but as long as I do not even know where the road to Buddha begins, or if it exists, I shall not wear it. Nor would I wear the swords of a Samurai."

Priest Jogen shook his head. "I think you will find the road one day, even if you never wear the robe of a priest. We must carry as little as possible. I have much to do before tomorrow."

I dressed myself in my own clothes once more and left the priest. I had little to collect for my journey. I made a bundle of the few spare clothes that I owned and my ink stone and the best of my brushes. On a sudden impulse I went to the shrine to Oinari-sama, the fox god who had protected me that long and cold winter. There was no one there, and the shrine looked even more dilapidated than it had when I lived under it. I rang the bell to tell the little god that a worshipper had come to ask a favor. "Oinari-sama, please protect us," I said, recalling the lady whom I had scared as she said her prayers. Although I did not believe in the little god, I felt better and more certain that we would succeed after making the visit to the shrine.

Priest Jogen had a box in his room in which he kept papers. I knew that among them were prayers he had written. Once I surprised him reading a prayer aloud, and he declared that such writing was but a sign of vanity and quickly put it away. In the back of the temple we had a place for burning refuse. I found the priest making a fire out of the box and its contents. I watched from a distance but did not approach. I felt sorry for him because he was the only one among us who stood to lose by our flight. To occupy myself I swept the temple. I was not sorry to leave but felt a little sad as I performed my duties in the knowledge that it was for the last time.

Priest Jogen was in excellent humor when I served our evening meal. It was but gruel with a little leftover rice from our breakfast. There had been no worshippers to leave bean curd or other gifts that day.

"Where shall we be sleeping tomorrow, Saru? Under the stars with a rock as a pillow and the moon as a lamp? It will not be the first time for me, but Murakami's wife is used to better."

"I think she will sleep more peacefully on the hard ground than she did between silk when she was a Takeda hostage. I wish tomorrow was here. I have made a bundle of what I shall take."

We have far to go and little time to get there. The less we

carry the better." Priest Jogen looked troubled. "What still worries me, Saru, is Murakami's wife. I fear she will be worn out before we have left Kofuchu."

"If we could buy a horse," I said, "she could ride."

"I have had the same thought, but to buy a horse is not that easy. I have no knowledge of such animals, and it is bound to be talked about. A poor priest buying a horse, I might as well buy a sword."

"Once we are outside the town, there may be a farmer who will sell us one," I suggested.

"Perhaps." The priest shrugged doubtfully. "Go and sleep, Saru, and tomorrow will tell its own story."

The night wrapped itself around me. The sky was cloudless and the stars very bright. It was now near the end of the eighth month of the year, the one said to be good for moon viewing. But there was no moon in the sky. Soon it would grow cold and another winter would come. Where would I live then? Where would be my home? As I lay down to sleep in my room I tried to imagine what the sea would be like. Water endlessly stretching as far, and farther, than your eyes could see. Almost as soon as I closed my eyes, the world disappeared and I slept.

29 *We Flee Kofuchu*

Though I had slept soundly, I woke early. Since I could not sleep again, I got up and washed my face. The sun had not yet risen, but the sky was light. To the southwest I could see Fuji-san. The mountain had a covering of snow on its very top, and the rising sun had turned it pink. By the hour of the dragon I had found myself a spot from where I could see the gate to the castle without being seen myself. As the hour of the snake grew near, I became more and more worried about what would happen. I imagined that our plot had long been discovered and that Shiro had already lost his head. He would have told about Priest Jogen and myself, and the soldiers would come to get us, too. It would all be my fault, my fault alone.

At the very moment when the hour of the snake began, I saw the litter. I watched it going though the gate, the two bearers running at a smart trot. The guards did not stop them. One of the soldiers even bowed as it passed.

Now I, too, ran and reached the temple before them. Luckily our alley was empty. Although the gate to the temple was never shut, I had made certain the night before that the two doors could be closed. As soon as the litter entered our yard, I shut the gates. Priest Jogen was there. He opened the litter and I held my breath, recalling my dream of the empty litter.

It was true that Murakami-san's wife was no taller than I, and it was also true that she was lovely. She was dressed in the most splendid of kimonos that I had ever seen. It was silk and had a crane embroidered on it. The crane is a symbol of longevity, and I thought it a good omen.

"The money!" Shiro demanded. I nodded and ran inside the priest's hut to get it for them. In the center of the room stood Murakami-san, his head bowed, and in front of him knelt his wife, her head touching the floor. They were as still as if they were carved in wood. Priest Jogen understood why I had come and handed me the two purses. I came out dazed by what I had seen, thinking that I had been right; they were different from us.

"The silver." Shiro's companion was older than he and a great deal rougher-looking. He eyed my purses greedily.

"There is a ruin of a house nearby where we can hide the litter," I commanded and ran to open the gates. For a moment I was not sure if they would follow me. Since I still held the money, they did. Our alley ended at the ruin, no more than fifty yards from our temple. The door had long been removed, and the opening was large enough for the litter to enter. Hidden from sight, it would take a while to find. When I handed over the purses, Shiro's companion tore his open and made a show of counting the pieces of silver. Shiro stuck his unopened purse inside his clothes and bowed to me. A moment later they had both disappeared.

In a time of war the countryside is filled with wandering beggars, farmers whose houses had been burned down, wounded soldiers no longer of use to their masters. "They will never get caught," I thought, "nor will anyone search for them." Our fate would be different. We could not count ourselves safe until we were well out of Kai, the Takeda province.

I hurried back to the temple and changed into my novice gown. Quickly I put my clothes into the bundle I had made the night before and I was ready.

When I entered the priest's hut a novice like myself turned around and stared at me. "This is Saru," Murakami-san said. I bowed and so did my double. Suddenly she laughed, and it sounded like little bells as she hid her mouth with her hand.

"We must hurry!" I said. "The litter is hidden, but who knows how soon they will start searching for it."

"We are ready." Priest Jogen looked at the Samurai, who took up his straw hat and put it on his head. His wife's hat was too big for her, and I wondered if she could see out under its brim. We each carried a bundle. Murakami-san's was long, so I guessed it hid his swords. I led them through the town I knew so well, choosing alleys and paths which were not often used and seldom, if ever, by Samurais. I hoped we would be taken for a group of pilgrims hurrying to some faraway temple to worship Buddha. Once I looked back and noticed that Murakami-san, who was walking beside his wife, carried himself straight whereas Priest Jogen walked with his head bent as if he were saying his prayers.

We did not stop until we were well out of the town. No one seemed to pay attention to us. Under the shade of a tree we sat down to rest. Murakami-san asked his wife if she was tired, and she shook her head. "We must not rest long," he said. His wife nodded in agreement, although, obviously, she was already tired.

"Let me carry your bundle," I said as we got up. For a moment I thought she was going to refuse, but then she smiled and handed it to me. "Monkeys are very strong and agile," Priest Jogen said. Murakami-san added that we were clever, too. I laughed and was the first back on the road.

By evening we had covered many ri and had met no one of any importance. We were looking for a place to rest and hide for the night when we suddenly heard the sound of horses approaching. Not far away some bushes were growing, tall enough to hide us. We rushed for them like hares which have spotted a hunter.

Through the leaves of the bushes we could see the road. It was a large group of mounted Samurais, half a hundred at least. I guessed that the leader was Takeda Katsuyori. His clothes were more splendid and his horse finer, as were its saddle and bridle. I glanced at Murakami-san, wondering what he felt as he watched his old comrades riding by. He had taken off his straw hat in order to see better. His expression was stern. Had he no longing to be among them again? Now he was merely a Ronin, a masterless Samurai, and once he buried his swords he would be even less. Behind the riders came a column of archers, their bows slung over their shoulders. Then the road was deserted again. After a long silence Murakami-san said what we had all been thinking: "That was Katsuyori."

Priest Jogen sat up and crossed his legs. "He will hear as soon as he is back in the castle."

"And tomorrow he will send out soldiers to pursue us." Murakami-san was looking in the direction of Kofuchu. "He will do so not because my head matters but because his pride demands it."

"We should walk farther as soon as the moon is up." Priest Jogen unfolded one of the bundles and took out the rice balls I had made the night before. I ate mine slowly, a lesson learned when I had been hungry. If you eat slowly you feel more satisfied than if you devour your food like a starving dog.

Murakami-san's wife was rubbing her feet. "Do they hurt?" I asked.

"They do. I am not used to walking. I think a bird which had long been kept in a cage would find its wings hurt when it is let out to fly." She looked up at me. Her face was beautiful. Her eyes were long and her nose more prominent than I was used to seeing. Her mouth was small like the bud of a flower.

"As soon as we get to the mountains we can rest. There, even if they pursue us, it is easier to hide. There will be cool pools to bathe our feet in when we are tired."

"Have you ever been to the mountains?" she asked, and I had to admit that I never had, nor ever bathed my feet in a cold mountain stream. She laughed and I joined in her laughter, knowing that we would become friends.

As soon as the moon had risen we continued our journey. We were walking in the direction of Lake Suwa, which is in the district of Shinano. The castle near the lake had belonged to Takeda Shingen. Oda Nobunaga conquered and destroyed it. From there to the sea we would have to pass through wild mountain country. However far we got that night, Lake Suwa would still be at least two days' march away.

30 *The Way of the Sword*

When the moon hid itself behind the mountains we rested once more. I slept for an hour or two, but as soon as the sky turned gray Priest Jogen woke me. "She is very tired, but we must go on. Those who pursue us will have horses." The Samurai was sleeping close to his wife. I touched his shoulder, and his hand went to where his obi and swords should be. Then he smiled. "I dreamed that Katsuyori himself was after us. But he will stay at home. Unlike his father he prefers to stay to the rear in a battle." Murakami-san leaned over his wife and touched her face gently. She looked at him, smiled, and sat up.

By noon even I was so tired that I threw myself on the ground in the shade of a large tree. My fellow novice sat down beside me. Removing her hat, she took the combs out of her hair and let it down. "How much farther do we have to go, Saru?" she asked.

"It is far to Lake Suwa, but beyond there we can rest. Priest Jogen talks of a small temple where it may be safe for us to spend a day or two."

"I was never very tall, but if we keep on like this I fear I shall become even smaller." She laughed and started to comb her hair and put it up again.

"Aki-hime, have you ever seen the sea?" I asked.

"Aki-hime? Oh, she died in Iwamura Castle. Aki will do from now on. As for the sea, I have never seen it. Some people say that big dragons live in it and when they fight, great waves are made."

"I have heard that it is wind which makes the waves. I do not think that I believe in dragons."

"Saru, my husband has told me that it is to you I owe my life. I thank you for it. I was terribly afraid of dying. Oh, it is not so much that I feared death but that I would not be able to face it with dignity and that my husband would be ashamed of me. I am not very brave."

The nearer we got to Lake Suwa the more lighthearted we became. The very day when we felt sure that we would reach the lake before sunset the worst happened. We didn't hear the sound of hooves until it was too late to run for cover. It was a lone Samurai. Priest Jogen dragged Aki into a field. Murakami-san drew his sword from his bundle and threw his hat down. The Samurai reined his horse only a few yards from us, then drew his sword.

"Murakami Harutomo, I have orders from Takeda Katsuyori to bring you back!" he declared.

"No doubt Katsuyori will give you a piece of gold for my head, but so far it still rests on my shoulders." Murakami-san looked at the Samurai in disgust. I recognized him as the one I had met near the house of the young robbers.

"Prepare to defend yourself!" the Samurai called. Spurring his horse, he trotted toward Murakami-san. As he passed he slashed at him, but Murakami-san jumped aside. The Samurai wheeled his horse, about to make another attack. "You have betrayed Takeda Katsuyori-sama and deserve death."

"And how many has Katsuyori betrayed? How many orphans and widows has he made?" I yelled.

"Who is this cockroach that dares speak to me?" the Samurai roared.

"My name is Saru, and we have met before."

"If we have met before I do not recall it, but I shall make certain that we shall never meet again."

"Let my wife and my companions alone and I shall follow you to Kofuchu." Murakami-san lowered his sword. Once more the Samurai spurred his horse and rode toward Murakami-san. As he passed me I dived for the horse, grabbed hold of the rein nearest me, and threw myself down. The horse whirled around and the Samurai's sword slashed down but missed me. I held on to the rein as the horse rose on its hind legs. When I saw its hooves thrashing above me I let go. I heard the clatter as the Samurai's sword fell to the ground as he tried to control the beast. On all fours I crawled the few steps to get it. When I stood up with the sword in my hand, I could not help laughing for the Samurai's face bore such a look of astonishment. "My sword!" he cried as he regained control of his horse.

"It is mine now!" I cried mockingly and swung it above my head.

"Give it back to him!" Murakami-san ordered.

"I will not," I answered furiously.

"You should not have interfered in our fight." Murakami-san stood in the center of the road, his sword poised. "If he gives you back your sword, I will fight you on foot."

"That is fair and honorable." The Samurai dismounted and walked toward me.

"What do you know of honor?" I screamed, suddenly so angry that I lost all control of myself. "If you come near me I shall kill you with your own sword."

"Your servant is ill brought up and knows little about behavior." The Samurai stopped a few feet from me.

"There was a Samurai who fled the castle and left his mother behind. Was he honorable? Your lord had her killed. Was that honorable? Maybe it was you who killed her. Was it?"

The Samurai lowered his had. "It was not I. A soldier strangled her."

"And like me he was so ill brought up that he did not know what honor was? I hate you Samurais and I hate you, too," I shouted at Murakami-san. I cast the sword toward him and ran as fast as I could away from them all. I threw myself in the grass beside the road. I was crying.

"Saru," a voice said near me. I did not look up. "You were right, and I beg you to forgive me. You know better what the word honor means than I do." I looked up at Murakami-san, who was kneeling beside me. I stared at him, then wiped my eyes with the back of my hand. "Do you still hate me, Saru-san?"

"I never did." I sat up and looked down the road. I could see Aki and the priest approaching. There was no sign of the Samurai. "What happened?" I asked.

"He has gone and will trouble us no longer." Murakami-san smiled.

"Did you kill him?"

Murakami-san shook his head. "He was too ashamed of losing his sword. I said I could not fight him in a robe dedicated to Lord Buddha. We gave him back his sword and he returned to Kofuchu. He will tell no one there, being too ashamed of having lost his sword to a monkey."

"That is good. I did not want him killed." I stood up and grinned toward Priest Jogen and Aki. I turned to Murakami-san. "I am honored that you called me Saru-san, but Saru fits me better."

"We shall be friends forever." Murakami-san pointed down the now deserted road. "That direction is the way of the sword. Ahead we may find, if not the road to Buddha, at least the path to peace."

"The roads in the mountains are steep and narrow, as is the way to Buddha. But if we walk without fear we shall get there." Priest Jogen looked solemn as he spoke.

"Let us rest in the temple you have talked about. I hope that the path there is neither steep nor narrow, for I am very tired." Aki pulled a funny face and put her hat on. We could not help laughing because she looked so comical in her large hat. Her husband declared that he was married to a walking mushroom.

31 *The Burial of the Swords*

It was another two days before we came to the temple in the mountains. The temple was very small, and only a priest and a novice lived there. Their statue of Buddha was old and poorly carved. The priest was small and fat. At the sight of him I thought we should eat well there. In this I was not wrong. He was good-natured and pleased to have company, new ears to pour old stories into. We arrived there late in the evening, and Aki was so tired that she fell asleep as soon as she had eaten. The rest of us sat up until the moon rose above the treetops; then we, too, were shown where to sleep. Murakami-san and his wife had a small room of their own while we shared the priest's room. The nights in the mountains are cold. There was not enough bedding for everyone, but I slept well under two old straw raincoats.

The priest kept hens, and in the morning we had eggs with millet porridge. We sat for a long time drinking tea and telling our host about our journey. I did not notice that Murakami-san had left. He had been silent while the rest of us were talking. When we finally finished, and I had washed the cups and dishes, I stepped outside. The sky was deep blue, and the outline of the mountains was drawn like a black line. I spied Murakami-san farther up the mountain, standing under a gnarled pine tree. A bird of prey, perhaps an eagle, sailed on the winds above us.

"Saru, I shall dig a grave here for my swords." Murakami-san smiled. "Then I shall cut my hair and Murakami Harutomo will be no more."

I nodded as if I agreed, although I did not! We could sell the swords. They would fetch a good price, and we might need the money.

"From now on call me Harutomo, just as I call you Saru. With the sword I bury the name that was my father's."

"When one becomes a priest one usually takes a new name," I said.

Murakami-san frowned. "I will let Priest Jogen give me a name and let him shave my head. The name Harutomo was given to me by Lord Akiyama Nobutomo. It was a precious gift and one which I shall miss." Murakami-san touched my shoulder. "Saru, whatever name I am given when I serve Buddha, you must still call me Harutomo, for from now on we are equals and friends."

"I will," I declared and laughed. "But I will always be Saru."

Harutomo-san dug a grave for his swords. It was hard for him to find a spot under the tree where the soil was deep enough. Late in the afternoon he carried his weapons up there and we all followed. Aki had a bundle, too. When Harutomo-san knelt to put the swords in the hole, Aki brought out the silk kimono. She wished it to be buried there, too. Harutomo-san hesitated for a moment, then wrapped the swords in the kimono and placed them in the grave. As he shoveled the earth, I caught a fleeting glimpse of the head of the crane embroidered on the kimono. I thought it very foolish. The kimono and swords were valuable enough to keep us all in food for a whole winter. Yet I was moved when I saw a tear run down Aki's cheek. Truly they are not like us. I glanced at Priest Jogen. His face was stern. Then I glanced at the fat and merry priest, our host, and I almost laughed aloud. His greedy little eyes were looking in wonder at the grave. It occurred to me that the grave would be robbed before we were out of sight.

We stayed for three days, until Aki had regained her strength. The priest gave us some food to take with us and refused the money that Priest Jogen offered him.

We set out in the early morning just as the sun had risen above the mountains. The path we followed was narrow and sometimes very steep. But we were happy. Now that we were well out of Kai, we walked without fear. The first night we slept in the mountains, or rather, we tried to sleep, but we were very cold, and as soon as there was light enough for us to follow the path we were up and away. The second night we came to a very small village where we were able to get both food and lodging for the night. The people were not friendly, and we decided to take turns to keep watch through the night. It was almost midnight when Priest Jogen woke me to say that it was my turn to keep watch. As he lay down to rest, he whispered in my ear: "Do you think the priest will steal the swords and the kimono, Saru?"

I grinned and nodded. "I think they have been sold already," I said.

"I think so, too. I wanted to warn him against it." Priest Jogen frowned. "Someone might suspect him of killing the owners. He could fare badly. There are Samurais who hate priests and would be quick to condemn him and carry out the sentence, too."

"If he stole them he is a thief," I whispered, glancing at the Samurai, whose head was now shaven like a Buddhist priest's. He was sound asleep beside his wife.

"It was but some iron and some cloth. A man's life is worth more than a silk kimono and two swords."

"I have known some who would kill for a few copper coins. But do not worry. He struck me as a man who—though greedy—would run no risk of losing his life."

"I hope you are right, Saru." Priest Jogen smiled. "He was a man who thought the road to Buddha went through his belly, but he was not bad."

"No," I whispered. "He was as most people are. He was lonely in that remote temple of his."

Priest Jogen nodded and gave me a staff he had cut on our way through the mountains. It was not a bad weapon should anyone try to break in and rob us.

I was so tired that it was hard for me to keep awake. Several times my head nodded and my eyes closed. Suddenly I heard someone near the sliding door to our room. I kept still. I was not far from the opening. The door slid back just enough for someone to climb through. I raised my staff and waited. Whoever was trying to get in was listening to hear if we were awake. A little moonlight filtered through a paper window. A head peeked through the doorway. At that moment Priest Jogen snored loudly and the intruder drew back. It was our host. He looked as frightened as a man entering a dragon's cave. When he had regained his courage, he crept in again. I waited until half of him was inside our room, then I struck him as hard as I could with my cudgel. He screamed and retreated, quickly closing the door behind him. I heard him moaning and the voice of his wife comforting him. I had no wish to do him any real harm. I thought it was the wife who had put the idea into his head. She had had a mean look in her eyes, and she had charged us too much for both meals and lodging.

The noise awoke everyone. Priest Jogen grabbed our purse, which he placed under his head. I could not help laughing at the expression on his face. "We had a guest," I said.

Harutomo jumped up and was looking for the swords he no longer had. Then Aki laughed, too, and soon we were all laughing.

The rest of the night passed peacefully. I was wakened by a dog barking. The sun had risen. The mountaintops were golden and the sky pale blue.

We left after a very skimpy breakfast served us by the wife. She excused her husband, saying that he was not well. We bowed and wished him good health and left the village. Often in such isolated places, people grow sour and mean. Left as they are to their own company, their only entertainment is to gossip about each other.

* * *

As we continued our journey through the mountains we saw a fox and, in the early morning, a Tanuki on its way home to sleep. The Tanuki is a mischievous little animal. They say that to become friends with one, you must offer it sake. As for the fox, I had always felt close to it since I had slept under its shrine. I was very pleased to have seen one.

32 *All Stories Must End*

It took us more than a week to cross the mountains. We had been traveling for ten days since we left the temple where Harutomo had buried his swords. Suddenly there were no more mountains in front of us. Instead a blue carpet stretched as far as we could see.

"That is the ocean," Priest Jogen said proudly. The day was calm and, like an enormous plain, it filled the world to the horizon.

"It is beautiful, but strange," Aki said. "It frightens me a little."

"It stretches all the way to the land where Buddha once walked." Priest Jogen smiled. "Not so far from here I was born. We still have some days to walk before we reach the temple where we will be welcome. You will find the people here more friendly than those we met in the mountains. They are poor but willing to share what little they have with a stranger. Most are both farmers and fishermen. Both land and sea are theirs."

"Both land and sea are theirs," Harutomo repeated. "But who is their lord?"

"I have heard that Maeda Toshiie now rules Noto. But where we are going, the lords seldom bother to come. The pickings are too lean. Our temple is on a peninsula that projects, like a bent finger, into the sea. There men have only two masters: the sea and the wind that whips the waves."

"Let us go to this land of yours." Harutomo looked at his wife. "Would you like a fisherman for your husband?" he asked with a smile.

Aki nodded, turned to the priest, and asked, "What does a fisherman's wife do?"

"She mends the nets he catches the fish in. I've often seen them hard at work, using both toes and fingers." Priest Jogen grinned and looked at me. "But what worries me is that the trees do not grow tall on the Noto peninsula. They may not suit a monkey to climb."

"I am a clumsy monkey that often falls down from trees. Maybe it is just as well that they are not too tall." From where we were standing the path descended like a snake toward the shore. I started downward and heard the others following me. I walked as fast as I could, for I wanted to be the first to reach the sea. Where the path was not too steep I ran and was down long before the others. The beach was covered with pebbles and larger stones. I took off my sandals and gingerly stepped into the water. Cupping my hands, I washed my face. Some of the water got into my eyes, and it hurt. I licked the skin of my hand. It tasted salty. A small fish nibbled at my feet. "I shall like it here," I thought as I moved my foot and the fish darted away.

* * *

It is strange how soon the unfamiliar becomes familiar. Before we had reached the temple by the sea, I had already become so used to the ocean that I felt as if I had always lived near it. The mountains are beautiful, but they are always the same. The sea is ever changing, like a living creature.

When we reached the temple which was to be our home, we were all worn out from traveling. The old priest gave us a cordial welcome. He was a kind old man, now a little blind and very deaf. The building stood on a low bluff overlooking the sea. The day we arrived it was calm and only the tiniest of waves lapped the shore. During the winter and spring storms, I got used to falling asleep listening to the howling of the wind and the drumming sound of great waves breaking against the shore.

"Does no one live here?" Harutomo asked. "It is the end of the world."

The old priest laughed. "We live here, and there is a village nearby. The houses are as poor as the people who live in them. They do not have much, but what they have they are willing to share. A young man came a few years ago, wanting to become a priest and stay here. He had been a novice at some great temple in Kai. He lasted one winter, and when spring came he left. He found the path to Buddha too stony here." The priest peered at Harutomo as if trying to gauge how long this newcomer would stay.

Harutomo-san shook his head. "A wise man or a fool may be happy here," he remarked.

"Then we shall be happy here. I shall be the fool and you the wise man," Aki whispered to her husband.

Harutomo-san looked at his wife and smiled. He touched her gently as he whispered in reply: "I shall try to become wise. If I can't you must be satisfied with having married a fool."

We have now lived here years enough for snow to fall on our hair. Have we become wise? I shall leave that question unanswered.

The old priest died a few years after we came, and Priest Jogen took his place. He, my friend, whom in my youthful arrogance I once deemed a fool, died two years ago. Harutomo is now the priest. For some years he and I did indeed own a boat and fished, so Aki-san did become a fisherman's wife. She, too, is dead now, and every once in a while when I see a certain smile on my friend's face I know he is thinking of her, and then I can hear Aki-san's laughter as lovely as a bird's song.

As for Takeda Katsuyori, he lived only a few months after we left Kofuchu. When the troops of Oda Nobunaga came, most of his soldiers deserted him, as did nearly all his friends. They say his wife was loyal to him to the end. His head was sent to Oda Nobunaga, who abused it and called him a fool. Nobunaga died not long after. Arrogance caused his death. He insulted one of his vassals, who killed him. Until recently Tokugawa Iyeyasu was shogun. When he died a few years ago his son Hidetada received the title.

But to us on our little peninsula, the high and mighty mean little. We remembered the years by the weather they held, not by the deeds of mighty lords. Five years ago we had a storm that nearly destroyed our temple, and many boats were lost. That is the sort of thing we consider of importance.

Thus I end the story of Saru the monkey. May whoever reads it find peace and contentment in life.